"Tell me, Maggie, how long you're staying."

Maggie lifted her chin and frowned. "Two weeks, not that it's any of your business."

"Oh, but it is." Galen reached out to tuck an errant strand of hair back from Maggie's face. "I want you to spend a day with me, going into the hills meeting some of the people I've told you about."

"I won't have time," Maggie said, trying desperately not to reveal the way she was trembling at being so close to Galen again, and feeling the excitement of his touch. "I want to spend all of my time with my father."

"Coward." Galen studied Maggie's face intently. "What are you afraid of? Me? What Roger might think? Or what you might find out about yourself?"

Katherine Arthur is full of life. She describes herself as a writer, research associate (she works with her husband, a research professor in experimental psychology), farmer, housewife, proud mother of five and a grandmother to boot. The family is definitely full of overachievers. But what she finds most interesting is the diversity of occupations the children have chosen—sports medicine, computers, finance and neuroscience (pioneering brain tissue transplants), to name a few. Why, the possibilities for story ideas are practically limitless.

Books by Katherine Arthur

HARLEQUIN ROMANCE

2755—CINDERELLA WIFE
2821—ROAD TO LOVE
2905—FORECAST OF LOVE
2948—SEND ME NO FLOWERS
2971—REMEMBER IN JAMAICA
2991—THROUGH EYES OF LOVE
3014—LOVING DECEIVER
3043—MOUNTAIN LOVESONG
3061—ONE MORE SECRET
3103—TO TAME A COWBOY

KEEP MY HEART FOREVER
Katherine Arthur

Harlequin Books

TORONTO • NEW YORK • LONDON
AMSTERDAM • PARIS • SYDNEY • HAMBURG
STOCKHOLM • ATHENS • TOKYO • MILAN

ISBN 0-373-03181-5

Harlequin Romance first edition March 1992

KEEP MY HEART FOREVER

CHAPTER ONE

THE BUS RATTLED ALONG, lurching from side to side with each turn of the road that wound through the ancient rounded mountains and deep narrow valleys of southern West Virginia. Maggie Preston shifted uncomfortably on the hard seat, wishing she had rented a car. The trip seemed much longer than she remembered. Each turn unfolded one more curve, opening yet another narrow valley before them, closing off the valley behind, like a receding tide pulling her ever deeper into the land she used to call home. Patches of melting snow lay flung like soggy rags between the leafless trees on the faded green hillsides. A dreary mist hovered low over the mountains and dripped from the eaves of a coal miner's cabin, slouched precariously beside a creek that was running bank full.

Maggie shuddered. The scene was familiar, and yet she felt like a stranger, so alien that if she were to stand in the middle of the road, the drivers of passing cars would have stared at her as if she had been dropped from another planet. At the bus station in Beckley, people had stared at her, but there had been no sign of recognition. People who took the bus to Spring Mountain did not read *Vogue* or buy the expensive cosmetics with which Maggie's distinctive heart-shaped face beneath its curly mane of flaming hair was identified. Their looks had been curious, wondering what an elegant-looking woman in a black coat with a blue fox collar could possibly be doing among the crowd wearing worn quilted jackets and jeans, their faces lined and tired from years of hard work. One tall man with coal-black hair had stared at her for an especially long time. He leaned on a metal cane, raking her up and down with his eyes, wide-set beneath sweeping black brows, one of which bore a slanted white scar. Even though he wore a quite presentable suit, his icy expression clearly condemned her for looking so affluent. Just another bitter injured miner, Maggie had thought, but the look stayed with her, isolating her even more.

I should have come home more often, Maggie thought, a feeling of desolate aloneness invading her. From the springboard of a modeling contest she had jumped onto the merry-go-round of success so swiftly that she had scarcely had time for a backward glance. In the past five years she had been home only twice. Once had been when her parents moved into the new home she had bought for them. The second time had been a year ago when she brought Roger Balfour to meet them. Her parents had wanted to meet the handsome, wealthy New Yorker whom Maggie mentioned so glowingly in her infrequent letters. Roger had borne up quite well, even though Maggie had felt uncomfortable at the way her father prodded him about the pollution the Balfour Chemical plant near Charleston, part of the empire that Roger controlled, might be causing.

"I hope Dad's questions didn't bother you, but he's been rabid on the subject ever since he developed black lung disease twenty years ago. It was too late for the new mine regulations to help him," Maggie had said later, as they flew back to New York in a company plane.

Roger had shrugged. "Not at all. It's quite understandable. Besides, you can't really expect someone who hasn't seen the business side of things to understand the complex decisions an owner has to make, balancing the environmental problems with the problem of turning a profit. As I told your father, we're doing everything that's legally required." Then he had quickly changed the subject to the opera they were going to see that night.

He really didn't like to have any contact with the unpleasant side of life, Maggie thought now with a frown. But her natural honesty led her to quickly admit to herself that she, too, usually felt more comfortable in the elegant brownstone in New York, which she had bought, on Roger's advice, as an investment. It was decorated in soft pastels, by a friend of Roger's, as a backdrop for her vivid coloring. In it, or at the opera, the ballet, the symphony or any of the numerous artistic events that Roger and his glittering circle of friends patronized, she felt like a fairy-tale princess, Cinderella rescued from the ashes. He delighted in her growing sophistication in the arts, which he cherished, making her feel as if she were living on a new and higher plane. But when she came home to West Virginia, she felt uneasy, like a traitor afraid of being discovered.

Maggie sighed heavily. She shouldn't blame Roger for his attitude. It wasn't his fault that he had never known poverty. And while her family had never been destitute, but had scraped by on her father's pension and the occasional housekeeping jobs her mother took on, she had known many children whose families were poor, and counted them among her friends.

There was a shuffling of feet as several passengers stood and removed parcels from the overhead rack, then sat down, leaning forward, poised to leave their uncom-

fortable seats as soon as possible. Maggie peered ahead
and saw in the distance the matchstick pattern of the
railroad trestle that crossed the Spring River at the nar-
rowest point in the valley. In that valley, nestled along
the side and base of a mountain, was the little town of
Spring Mountain. Home.

Maggie felt her pulse quicken in a combination of anticipation and dread. *Don't borrow trouble,* she told
herself firmly. Wait and see how things really are. In the
invitation to her parents' thirty-fifth wedding anniversary celebration, the event that was bringing Maggie
home, her mother had added a little postscript: "The
way your father's health is, I don't know how many
more there will be." Knowing that her mother had been
none too subtly telling her that her father's health was
failing had filled Maggie with a sense of foreboding, accompanied by a feeling of guilt for neglecting her adored
father in recent years. Even though she reminded herself that her parents reveled in her success and appreciated all that her money had done for them, the feeling
would not go away.

When the bus came to a stop before the dingy little
frame building that served as both bus depot and restaurant, Maggie followed several other passengers to the
door. Her feet had scarcely touched the ground when she
was swept into a bear-hug embrace and swung off her
feet. "How's my beautiful sister?" said a laughing,
boyish voice.

"Bruce!" she shrieked. "Put me down!" When he
complied, she gazed into the bright blue eyes of her
brother then flung her arms around him and kissed him.
"You look wonderful," she said, drawing back to see
him better. "Just wonderful. And prosperous, too. That
leather trench coat is very becoming."

Bruce shrugged and looked pleased. "I can't complain. I've been made chief accountant at Balfour Chemicals." He laughed as Maggie's mouth fell open in surprise.

"How marvelous!" she exclaimed, hugging him again. "Roger didn't tell me. That beast. He never tells me anything about his businesses, but he could at least have told me that."

"I told him to let me tell you in person," Bruce said, picking up Maggie's suitcases as the bus driver pulled them from the baggage compartment. He gave her a quick self-satisfied grin. "Come and see my new toy," he said, starting toward the parking area.

"Wow!" Maggie stared dumbfounded at the bright red Ferrari that Bruce stopped beside. "That is some toy," she said, touching its gleaming fender appreciatively.

"Nice, huh?" Bruce agreed, opening the door for her. "And wait until you see my new digs," he added as he got in beside her. "I just moved into a new condo development on the edge of Charleston. Artificial lake, swimming pool, tennis courts. And the apartment's got a built-in speaker system in every room, a Jacuzzi, and a kitchen you wouldn't believe. It's the perfect bachelor pad. And with this car..." He grinned and gave Maggie a broad wink.

"You must cut quite a swath," Maggie said, smiling at him. She fastened her seat belt and held her breath as Bruce roared off, driving as if he was in a road race through the hills of the little town. Bruce was obviously enjoying the fruits of his labors to the hilt, she thought. There was no reason for her to feel guilty about enjoying hers, also.

Bruce careered around an uphill corner at the end of a road then brought his car to a gravel-spraying stop before the house on a new little cul-de-sac at the highest edge of Spring Mountain, where the elder Prestons now lived. Maggie looked at the house and smiled in satisfaction. The sight of the sprawling brick ranch house, with its large picture windows overlooking the valley, gave her renewed confidence in the value of her own success. Here, deer frequently came wandering into the backyard from the thickly wooded mountainside just beyond the border of her mother's meticulously tended gardens. It was a far cry from the small wooden house on a tiny treeless lot, just barely on the right side of the railroad tracks in Spring Mountain, where she and Bruce had grown up.

At the sound of the car door opening, Maggie's attention was jerked back to the here and now, and the reason for her anxiety about coming home. "Wait," she said, putting her hand on Bruce's arm before he could get out. "How's Dad? Really?"

Bruce looked down then at Maggie. Beneath his thatch of dark red hair, his boyish face looked hard and angry. "I didn't know quite how to bring this up," he said, "but I expect it's better if I do instead of letting you walk into a hornet's nest."

"Hornet's nest? I don't understand," she said. "I thought from what Mom wrote that Dad's health was worse."

"Well, it is and it isn't," Bruce said, looking down again and frowning. "He needs to have oxygen more often now and he seems pretty listless at times, but the doctor says there isn't that much change in his lung condition. I think the real problem is that he's not all that keen on your marrying Roger Balfour anymore."

He gave Maggie a quick appraising glance. "How's that deal coming along? You got him pinned down yet?"

"I don't know if that's quite the way I'd put it," Maggie said, "but Roger told me we'd be looking at diamonds when I get back to New York, and I'm not to put him off anymore. I guess you'd call that pinned down. What's the problem?" She could see that Bruce was seething with some unspoken fury.

The fury exploded, Bruce's eyes flashing with an angry hostility. "It's that damned Galen Kendrick! He's the lawyer for an environmental group that's making all kinds of wild accusations against Balfour Chemicals. He's been over and talked to Dad, and of course he believes every stupid lie that Kendrick tells him. I've tried to talk some sense into Dad, but he's sure now that Roger Balfour is the same kind of irresponsible monster that the mine owners were forty years ago. You and I know better. My God, he's a terrific guy."

Maggie frowned. "That certainly puts a damper on things, doesn't it? How does Mom feel about it?"

Bruce grimaced. "She's with Dad, as usual. It might be just as well if you soft-pedal your relationship with Roger while you're here. Keep things going smoothly." A harsh coldness that Maggie had never seen before turned Bruce's usually soft-looking features stony. "We'll get that damned Kendrick off of our backs before too long. He doesn't know that he's playing with the big boys now."

"I'll keep it vague," Maggie promised, in spite of the shuddery feeling she got at Bruce's veiled threat. She and Galen Kendrick had been fast friends once long ago, when he had been badly injured in a crash, driving a car that she remembered as an earlier version of Bruce's. She had been making some extra money reading his lessons to him, when his poor bandaged hands were useless and his eyes were barely visible between layers of tape. Later, when he had been able to go back to school in a wheelchair, still waiting for reconstructive surgery on his face, his former friends had shunned him. He had become quiet and serious, his brush with death making him instantly older. Even though he was actually several years older than she was, they had spent long hours discussing, with what passed for profundity in their teens, the meaning of life. She was not surprised to hear that he had become an advocate for something he felt deeply about.

"How is Galen now?" Maggie asked as they got out of Bruce's car. "I mean physically," she added, as Bruce gave her a sharp look. "Is he still in a wheelchair? Did he get his face repaired?"

Bruce's mouth twisted unpleasantly. "Oh, yeah. His face looks okay. And he can get around with only a cane, which I doubt he really needs. I think he uses it for its effect on a jury. Gets instant sympathy for his side."

Maggie raised her eyebrows but said nothing. Inside she felt a sudden turmoil. That man in Beckley who'd stared at her—it had been Galen Kendrick! She should have recognized those wide-set gray eyes, that scar across his brow, even though the face that surrounded them was now almost handsome; and standing tall, staring down at her with contempt, he had a very different appearance than she had remembered. Why had he looked at her like that? Did he think she knew who he was and didn't speak because she felt she was too good to speak to an old friend? For that matter, why didn't he speak to her if he recognized her, as he surely must have?

Just then the door of the house swung open. "Are you two going to stand out there all day talking?" Mrs. Preston called, holding her arms open in welcome.

"Hi, Mom!" Maggie called as she smiled and waved, relieved to see that her mother looked the same. Except for the graying curls, she was still the slightly plump figure, perennially wearing an apron tied over her dark slacks and colorful top, that Maggie had always run to when things went wrong. Maggie ran up the sidewalk and into her encompassing embrace. "It's so good to see you," she said, hugging her tightly and kissing her smooth cheek. She even smelled just right, a blend of roses and spice that had always spelled warmth and security.

Mrs. Preston broke away from Maggie's tight embrace and held her at arm's length. "My goodness, you look elegant," she said. "How did this poor little town ever produce such a beautiful flower?"

"Now, Mom, don't get carried away," Maggie said, laughing. She turned to greet her father and had trouble keeping the smile on her face. In the year since she'd seen him, he seemed to have aged a decade. Gone forever was the brawny red-haired man, proud of his strength, who had come home from the mines each day covered in coal dust to swing his little daughter high over his head and laugh when she squealed with delight. All that remained were the bright blue eyes that Maggie and Bruce had inherited, in a body so fragile-looking that Maggie feared he might crumble if she held him too tightly. She quickly flung her arms around him and buried her face in his shoulder. "It's so good to see you, Dad," she said hoarsely.

"Good to have you here, love," her father said, patting her back. "And I'd say it's not a flower but a precious jewel we have in our midst. It's going to be a real treat to be able to show you off at the party tomorrow."

"And I'd say you're both sweet but very prejudiced," she said, gaining control of herself and raising her face to receive his kiss, hoping the tears in her eyes would pass for tears of joy. "I hope you don't plan to embarrass me with that kind of flowery praise tomorrow. I'm just a hillbilly who made good."

"Oh, come on, Maggie," Bruce said, looking annoyed. "You make it sound like we were a bunch of barefoot illiterates who ate possum for dinner."

"Well, something smells wonderful. What's for dinner? Possum pie?" Maggie asked, giving Bruce a cold look. He sounded almost as snobbish as some of Roger's friends, who looked first surprised and then appalled when she told them where she was from. "My goodness, Spring Mountain, West Virginia. Really?" they would say. "Is that near Charleston? Or the Greenbrier?" Then, when she told them it was a small mining town in the hills and she was a coal miner's daughter, they would simply stare in disbelief. Roger suggested she might better omit that detail, but Maggie kept doing it, getting a perverse pleasure out of watching their awkward efforts to cover their distress.

"Not tonight," Mrs. Preston said with a little smile, having quickly caught the undercurrent between her children. "It's a simple goulash. I had so much cooking to do for the party tomorrow that I didn't have time to fix anything that fancy."

"Darn," Maggie said, pretending to be disappointed.

Bruce smirked. "Ha, ha. So, where do you want these suitcases, or am I supposed to stand here holding them all night?"

"The bedroom with the blue wallpaper," Mrs. Preston replied.

"Do I have time to change before dinner?" Maggie asked. "I feel all gritty from that bus ride."

"Go ahead. No rush," her mother replied. "Take a shower if you want."

Maggie quickly showered and slipped into comfortable gray slacks and a soft blue sweater. "Now I feel human again," she said as she returned to the kitchen and watched her mother begin to put the dinner on the table in the breakfast room next to the kitchen. Its bow window overlooked a pleasant patio surrounded by rhododendrons that would be covered with spectacular pink blooms in the spring. "Let me help. I don't like feeling useless," she said.

"You'll have plenty to do tomorrow," her mother said with a shake of her head. "Call your father. He's probably dozing in front of the TV."

In the adjoining TV room, Maggie found her father, as predicted, reclining in a lounge chair, his head slumped to one side, the news program ignored. "Dinner's on the table," she said, awakening her father with a kiss on the top of his balding head. "May I escort you?"

"Anytime, love," he replied, smiling and getting slowly to his feet. He put his arm around her. "It's so good to have you home. I'm glad your mother finally thought of a way to get you here for a while, even if I do have to put up with a houseful of friends and relations tomorrow. Two weeks you said you can stay?"

Maggie nodded, a sudden tightness in her throat making it difficult for her to speak. She was going to have to make a lot more time in her busy schedule to come home from now on.

The four of them sat down to a dinner that featured the beef-and-macaroni goulash that Maggie remembered had been a favorite staple of their diet for many years. "I'm going to have to get the recipe for this to give to Anna," she said, smiling at her mother. "Ever since I sent her to cooking school, she tends to overdo the sauces. She seems to have forgotten how to do anything that's really simple and delicious."

"Sometimes simpler is better," her mother said with a pleased smile.

"Must be nice to have a cook," Bruce said enviously. "I get tired of takeouts and TV dinners."

"Learn to cook yourself. I did before I could afford Anna," Maggie suggested.

"I'm too busy," Bruce replied, and Maggie could see from the distant look in his eyes that he was mentally calculating how much more he would have to make before he could have his own cook. He was going to have trouble, she thought ruefully, coming anywhere close to her income. It was too bad he seemed to think he had to compete.

When her mother asked—rather hesitatingly, Maggie noticed—about how she and Roger were getting along, Maggie shrugged and said, "Oh, just fine," then quickly changed the subject to the party the next day.

"It's going to be an open house and buffet, starting at noon," her mother said. "I expect some people will stop by right after church, and others may wait until later. I've got enough food ready to feed an army, but we'll have to keep hopping to make sure there's always plenty on the table."

"Who all are coming?" Maggie asked.

"Oh, goodness, let me see," said her mother, pausing thoughtfully. She ran through a list of aunts and uncles and cousins, townspeople and old friends of her father's. But when she mentioned the name Galen Kendrick, Bruce interrupted loudly.

"What in the devil did you have to invite him for?" he demanded.

"Why, because I thought Maggie would like to see him," Mrs. Preston replied, giving her son a reproving look. "Just because you and he disagree doesn't mean we can't invite him to our house."

"I doubt that Maggie wants to see him, either," Bruce said, giving Maggie a meaningful look. "I told her about his being out to get Balfour Chemicals with a bunch of crazy charges."

"I'd still like to see him," Maggie said, catching a dangerous flash from her father's eyes and frowning at her brother. She wasn't at all sure that Galen wanted to see her, but she definitely would like to find out why he had looked at her as if she was a particularly contemptible specimen.

"There, you see?" Mrs. Preston said. She turned toward Maggie. "It's been a long time, hasn't it? You'll be surprised at what a fine-looking man Galen is now. You can hardly tell he had that terrible accident when he was a boy."

"How nice," Maggie said, while in her mind's eye she was picturing the man she had seen, that high-cheekboned, angular face with the hawkish nose. It was definitely a memorable face. Fine-looking, maybe, if he hadn't looked as if he'd like to bite her.

"Tell us about that trip you made to Fiji last month," her father suggested tactfully. "Is it really paradise?"

"Close to it," Maggie replied. She obligingly began a detailed description of the lovely islands where she had spent several weeks being photographed in next summer's fashions, but she could see that Bruce was still angry. Strange, she thought, that he had so completely adopted the industry viewpoint. She would have expected him, considering their father's misfortune, to remain at least neutral. Apparently his rapid and successful rise at Balfour Chemicals, and perhaps even some of Roger's personal persuasive charm, had made him a real convert.

After dinner, Maggie talked to her father a little longer, but he tired quickly. She watched sadly as her mother helped get the oxygen tube fitted to his nose once he was in bed.

"Darned nuisance," he grumbled, "but it helps me sleep better." He patted the edge of his bed. "Sit down and give me a good-night kiss," he ordered.

Maggie sat and bent to kiss him, then laid her head on his shoulder. He patted her fiery curls and sighed. "Seems like just yesterday I used to tuck you into bed at night."

"I know," Maggie said softly. It did seem such a short time ago. Suddenly all the years between seemed to telescope into a brief but vivid dream that had not really happened at all. She raised her head and smiled at her father. "I'm going to spend a lot more time here from now on," she said. "I've missed you."

Her father wrinkled his nose and eyed her suspiciously. "Now, don't you go fussing over me and stop doing what you're doing because you think I'm falling apart. I love you, and I like to have you here, but I want you to be happy most of all." He paused and looked uncomfortable. "How are things going with you and that Balfour fellow?" he asked.

Maggie shrugged, glad that Bruce had warned her. "Still nothing definite," she said lightly. Her father's relief was ill concealed, although his words were carefully neutral.

"I'm glad to see you're taking your time about such an important decision," he said.

"Mom always said, marry in haste, repent at leisure," Maggie told him with a smile. "Good night. See you in the morning."

It was early when Maggie went to bed. She wanted to get away and be alone, finding something in Bruce's company disturbing. He looked every inch the rising young professional, in his pink cashmere sweater, gray pleated slacks and British loafers, not in itself a condemnation. It was, she decided, his implicit attitude that he was now better than most people. When she commented on his stylish clothes, he made snide remarks about the local clods and took pains to say that Galen Kendrick, whose family was by far the wealthiest in Spring Mountain, dressed in cheap, ill-fitting suits. Maggie had to bite her tongue to keep from remarking that Bruce might not have fared so well if it weren't for her connection with Roger Balfour, a fact that Bruce seemed easily to forget.

As for herself, Maggie thought as she lay awake staring into the quiet darkness, she felt decidedly, uncomfortably, off balance, like a person on skates for the first time who lurches madly forward and backward, then finally falls on her behind. Who was she, really? The glamorous woman in jewels and designer originals who pouted prettily from the pages of fashion magazines? Or the scrawny teenager in faded jeans and tattered tennis shoes who had sat for hours talking to the battered Galen Kendrick, enthralled with his mind and barely noticing his scars?

"I must be having an identity crisis," she muttered to herself. Trying to go home to a long-abandoned life-style sometimes did that to people. She would feel better when she was in New York. Meanwhile, she had better get some sleep so she could be her parents' little flower and jewel in the morning.

SHE HAD LITTLE TIME to ponder any contrasts in the morning. There were festoons to hang across the dining room like a canopy, centered on the crystal chandelier, and balloons to blow up and fix in clusters by the windows. When that was done, there were platters of sliced roast beef, ham and turkey, baskets of breads, bowls of homemade pickles and condiments to put out on the table. A huge bowl of punch was placed on the buffet. Her father wandered around, trying to keep track of her, until she led him to his favorite lounge chair in the living room and said firmly, "You stay put! It's going to be a long afternoon."

"I think you're going to need some of my oxygen if you don't slow down," he teased.

"Keep it handy," Maggie replied with a grin.

She had just helped carry the huge, decorated anniversary cake to the table when the clock chimed noon.

"You'd better change your clothes, Maggie," her father said. "I expect some of the folks will come by right after church."

"Oh, Dad, do I have to?" Maggie whined, standing in front of him and feigning a terrible teenager's pout.

Her father laughed so hard that he began to cough. "Damn!" he said hoarsely. "I hope nobody tells me any really good jokes this afternoon."

"Bruce, make a sign," Maggie said to her brother, who had come to see if his father was all right. "Draw a circle with the words 'good jokes' in the middle and a line drawn through it. We'll hang it on Dad's chair.'' When her father started to chuckle again, she frowned at him in mock severity. ''Stop that, or I won't change my clothes.'' Then she gave him a kiss and ran to her room, blinking the mist from her eyes. What a horrible affliction, not to be able to laugh as hard as you wanted to! She paused in the middle of stripping off her clothes. Come to think of it, she had never heard Roger laugh really hard. She had thought that his controlled chuckle was a sign of refinement, but maybe it was only that he didn't find anything very funny. That would be even worse than not being able to laugh.

Maggie put on her makeup with the quick expertise of years of practice, then slipped into a simple periwinkle-blue jersey dress with long sleeves and a surplice bodice. She wore no bra to spoil the smooth lines, only the filmiest of silk panty hose beneath it. With it she wore the diamond-and-sapphire pendant earrings, slender necklace of diamonds supporting another sapphire and diamond pendant that Roger had had Tiffany's make especially for her. ''To complement the blue of your eyes,'' he'd said.

When she returned to the living room, several guests had already arrived and more were coming up the walk to the front door. Maggie was kept busy greeting old friends, trying desperately to remember who many of them were without giving her forgetfulness away and graciously responding to the many overblown congratulations on her success.

''I'll bet Kendrick isn't going to show up,'' Bruce remarked in an undertone as their paths crossed. ''It's almost three o'clock.''

Maggie shrugged and tried to look indifferent. The truth of the matter was that she knew exactly what time it was, and for the past hour had been looking quickly toward the door every time it opened. She was haunted by the image of the look he had given her yesterday, made even more disturbing by her conjuring of images of an earlier time, when there had been warmth in his startlingly wide-set gray eyes and a crooked smile on that sadly damaged face. She had decided to greet him with her most dazzling smile when he came, and apologize profusely for not recognizing him in hopes of breaking the ice.

She was sitting on the arm of her father's chair, conversing with him and one of his former co-workers, when she began to feel a prickling in the back of her neck, as if someone was watching her. She turned slowly and looked around. There, standing in the doorway to the dining room, devouring her with those huge gray eyes, was Galen Kendrick. He was wearing a beautifully tailored suit of dark gray that fit his broad shoulders to perfection, and above his white shirt, his swarthy coloring and arrestingly angular but not quite symmetrical features gave him a look of tremendous yet well-contained power. Maggie's pulse began to race, and her face spontaneously broke into a wide smile.

"Galen!" she said, getting up from her seat in one fluid movement and going toward him, her hands outstretched. "I didn't recognize you yesterday. It took me a while to realize it was really you. You look absolutely marvelous. I'm so glad to see you." She kept smiling as she reached his side, even though as she drew near she watched his expression become guarded, almost cold. He lifted his chin and looked down his hawkish nose at her, unsmiling.

"It's nice to see you, too, Maggie," he replied, taking her hands only briefly. "I'm sure I'm not the first to tell you how beautiful you look and congratulate you on your success."

Maggie's smile faded and she studied him curiously. His voice had a flat tinge of irony, and although he did not look as openly hostile as he had the day before, she had the feeling he was trying to cover up his feelings with a stoic mask and was not altogether succeeding. She raised her chin and returned his cool stare. "No, you're not," she replied, "but I had hoped you'd come up with something more original. You always were quick-witted, and I understand you're a very successful lawyer now."

The dark fringe of Galen's lashes lifted momentarily, giving Maggie a glimpse into a sea of frigid gray. "Maybe I'm just too dazzled to think of anything better," he suggested in slightly mocking tones. "I'd have thought you'd be used to that."

Two can play this game, Maggie thought. She lowered her chin, widened her eyes and treated Galen to the evil pussycat smile she sometimes used in sexy swimwear photographs. "Why, of course," she purred sarcastically. "I get most of my exercise stepping over the bodies of the men who fall at my feet."

One black eyebrow jerked upward, and the icy look returned full force. "Too bad you didn't step over Roger Balfour," he said, "or did the sparkle of the diamonds he threw in your path blind you so that you tripped and fell?" His eyes raked from her face to her jewels and back.

"My God," Maggie murmured, staring at him, dumbfounded. That was way beyond the rules of verbal repartee. What right did this man, whom she hadn't seen in almost nine years, have to make a remark like that?

"I don't believe that deserves an answer," she said with a look that would have frozen most men on the spot.

Galen seemed unfazed. "I wonder," he said with an appraising look, "if that's because Balfour is so hard to defend, or is it something else? You used to be fairly quick-witted, too, but I've heard that hedonism dulls the senses."

Maggie's mouth fell open and it took her several moments to regain her powers of speech enough to spit out under her breath, "You are the most disgustingly rude man I have ever met!" With that, she turned and walked away, afraid that if she listened to one more of Galen Kendrick's rude remarks she would slap his face. Behind her, she heard a deep throaty chuckle and knew he was laughing at her.

She was still seething when Bruce drifted up beside her at the punch bowl. "You look like storm clouds gathering," he said in an undertone. "Renewed your acquaintance with Kendrick?"

"Uh-huh," Maggie replied over the edge of her punch cup. She swallowed then gave the cup a disgusted look. "I wish I was more of a drinker. Then I'd have something stronger than this fruit punch."

"Charming, isn't he?" Bruce smiled wryly and looked toward the living room. "Like a python."

For the first time since Maggie had turned her back on him, she looked in Galen Kendrick's direction. He had drawn a chair up close to her father's and was leaning back comfortably, gesturing with one large, long-fingered hand as he spoke. Once again, Maggie had a sense of his dominating presence. Even in a room full of CEOs of giant corporations like Roger Balfour, he would stand out. He seemed to sense her staring at him and looked up. An amused smile barely crinkled the corners of his eyes, and Maggie looked quickly away, her cheeks burning.

"His suit fits," she remarked to Bruce irrelevantly.

"I noticed. Must be a new one," Bruce replied. He bent his head closer to Maggie's ear. "He's a dangerous man. He seems to think that God's anointed him to save the world and every misbegotten piece of humanity in it, and the devil take anyone who disagrees with him."

"I had noticed a certain judgmental quality," Maggie said dryly. She shot another glance in Galen's direction then kept on looking. He was leaning forward now, something humorous apparently passing between him and his father, for they were both grinning broadly in a man-to-man sort of way. She turned toward Bruce, but the image of that smile stayed with her, white teeth flashing, framed in lines that gave it an added dimension of warmth. A smile that could make women fall at his feet if he ever deigned to use it on them. "Is he married?" she asked.

Bruce shook his head and gave Maggie a sly smile. "Too bad he isn't. You could use your wiles to break it up. That might send him on a real downer."

"I don't like that idea," Maggie said, giving Bruce a sharp look. "I'm surprised you'd suggest it, and I can imagine what Roger would think of it."

"Oh, come on, Maggie," Bruce scoffed. "You must know Roger better than that. If he thought it would be good for business, he'd go for it in a minute."

Maggie felt her temper rising again. "Are you suggesting that Roger is amoral?" she demanded. "Because if you are, you're very much mistaken. Roger is the most perfect gentleman I've ever met. He's never even..." She stopped, not wanting to bring up anything too revealing about her personal relationship with

Roger Balfour. She could tell by Bruce's knowing grin that she had already gone too far.

"He knows how to get what he wants," Bruce said.

The thought that Roger might have dimensions completely unknown to her gave Maggie a cold, unpleasant feeling, as if she had just stumbled into a dim cavern full of shadowy unseen forces. She was glad to turn her attention to answering her mother's call to come and meet an old friend.

"You remember Mrs. Collins, don't you?" her mother said, her arm around a small, rotund woman with springy white curls and cheeks like polished apples. "Your second-grade teacher?" she added as a prompt when she saw the confusion in Maggie's eyes.

"Of course," Maggie said, taking the woman's hand while she tried desperately to send her mind back twenty years. "Weren't you the one who jumped on her desk when I brought the nest of baby field mice to school in a box?"

"The same," said Mrs. Collins with a smile. "I never thought you'd grow up to be such a beauty. In fact, you got into so much mischief that I wasn't sure you'd grow up at all. The worst tomboy I ever saw. And such a temper."

"I was pretty awful, wasn't I?" Maggie said, laughing. It had been a long time since she had thought that far back, to the days when she hated to put on a dress or shoes for fear she'd get stuck playing dolls with the girls when she really wanted to be playing cowboys and Indians with the boys.

They fell into an easy discussion of that time, Maggie quickly learning that she had made quite an impression on poor Mrs. Collins, most of it not very favorable. For some reason, it seemed a pleasant antidote to all the flattering attention she had been receiving from everyone. Everyone, of course, but Galen Kendrick, whose presence she had mercifully been able to ignore—except when his deep masculine laugh rang out and reminded her that he was still there and obviously not treating anybody else like a pariah. Each time she heard it she felt angry, which was, she thought, a stupid response. If he wanted to be nasty to her, let him. He was only a minor annoyance. A worm in the apple of life, as her mother used to say. Besides, if she really kicked him in the shins, as she felt like doing, it would probably only hurt her toe.

As the crowd began to thin out, several other people, including some cousins whom Maggie had not seen in a long time, joined the pleasantly reminiscing group. Suddenly their quiet conversation was interrupted by loud voices from the next room.

"Balfour Chemicals has done more good for the state of West Virginia than you and that crazy bunch of environmental busybodies will ever do!" Bruce said shrilly.

"You've got a strange definition of good," came Galen's calm reply, his voice deep and low but resonant with carefully curbed passion. "Since when are cancer and damaged nervous systems good? How many people will have to die before you'll call what Balfour does bad?"

"Oh, spare me your tragic statistics," Bruce spat contemptuously. "Try and convert some other mindless fools to go around waving your banners. You can't prove a damned thing! You're nothing but a . . ." He finished the sentence with such a stream of vulgarity that Maggie could scarcely believe her ears.

"Bruce! Stop that!" her father's voice interrupted loudly. Then he went into a violent coughing spell.

Ellen Preston rushed to her husband's side and picked up the small portable oxygen mask that sat on the table by his chair while Maggie fairly flew to confront her brother.

"You dimwit!" she snapped, glaring at Bruce, who was still glaring, red-faced, at Galen. "Now look what you've done. Get out of here and take a walk until you cool off. Now. I mean it!"

For a moment, Bruce looked as if he was going to make a sharp retort to Maggie, but after surveying her flashing eyes and angrily set jaw he shrugged, gave her a defiant look and walked off toward the TV room.

Maggie turned her attention to Galen. "You're not blameless, either," she said coldly. "You knew what would happen if you needled Bruce, didn't you? Couldn't you stay off that missionary high horse of yours for one afternoon just to keep things running smoothly?"

"No," Galen replied, fixing Maggie with a look that seared through her own anger and left it in futile shreds. "And neither could most people who've seen what I've seen." He accented the "most people" with an inflection and a meaningful lift of his heavy dark brows.

"Most people?" Maggie frowned. "Who are you excluding? Are you implying that Bruce has seen what you have and doesn't care?"

Galen shook his head. "He's seen nothing. He doesn't want to. It seems to run in the family."

Once again, Maggie's mouth fell open in shocked surprise, but this time she lost no time in replying loudly, "I think that's about enough of your groundless accusations. You've done nothing but attack me ever since you came into this house, and I've had enough of it. Where do you get the idea that you can get away with—" She stopped, biting her lip, as her mother called her name, feeling a little foolish that being called "Margaret" still intimidated her. "I am not sorry and I don't apologize, except for raising my voice," she said more softly, scowling at the amused look on Galen's face.

"Maybe we should take a walk so that you can yell at me as loudly as you want," Galen suggested. "I'm rather curious about how you got to be the way you are."

"The way—" Maggie began, her temper flaring again. She didn't finish, thinking that perhaps she should go somewhere where she could really give Galen Kendrick a piece of her mind without shocking the remaining guests. But there was a lot of cleaning up to do as soon as the guests were gone, and she could hardly leave her mother alone to cope with it. "I'd love to tell you exactly what I think of how *you've* gotten to be," she said, "but I have to help my mother clean up the mess. Besides, I can't go walking in high heels."

"I'll have plenty of help," Mrs. Preston said, having listened in on the conversation from a few feet away. "Aunt Martha and Helen said they'd stay and help out. Go ahead."

"Change your shoes," Galen said in a tone that was more like an order than a suggestion.

Maggie shrugged and walked away. In the hallway she found Bruce talking to their cousin Keith.

"What's up?" Bruce asked. "The party over?"

"Not exactly," Maggie replied. "I'm going to take Galen Kendrick outside and give him a piece of my mind."

"Good girl," Bruce said with an approving nod. "Just be sure he doesn't start twisting your mind around to his point of view."

Keith grinned. "You've got to give the guy credit, being willing to take on Roger Balfour's fiancée."

"I am not Roger's fiancée yet," Maggie said. "And Galen's views are not what I want to talk about. Excuse me." She pushed past the two men and went into her room, where she kicked off her pumps and quickly tied on a pair of walking shoes. They might not look chic with her dress, but she was not going to waste time changing. Nor was she going to take off the jewelry that seemed to offend Galen. It wasn't her fault that Roger delighted in giving her such trinkets, nor that he had the money to do so. They didn't give Roger any particular leverage over her. If she decided not to marry him, she would give them back. She grabbed her coat off the hanger in her closet, slung it over her shoulder and hurried to the living room.

"I'm ready," she said to Galen, who was leaning against the dining-room door frame, his cane in hand, smiling engagingly at Mrs. Collins.

"So am I," he replied, giving Maggie a quick glance. Then he bent and gave Mrs. Collins a kiss on her cheek. "Take care, Nell," he said, "and be sure and come by my office next time you're in Charleston. We'll have coffee and talk some more."

He straightened as Mrs. Collins beamed and said, "I will. You take care, too, dear."

Anyone would think he was running for public office, kissing babies and little old ladies, Maggie thought irritably. He took Maggie's coat from her hand.

"Liberated enough to not wear a bra, but not liberated enough to put on your own coat?" he murmured into her ear as he held it for her.

It was all that Maggie could do to keep from jerking the coat away from him. Instead she gave him an icy glare. "It must be a terrible trial for you, pretending to be a gentleman," she retorted, then opened the door and hurried outside ahead of him.

CHAPTER TWO

WHEN MAGGIE reached the end of the sidewalk she turned and waited for Galen, her hands thrust deep in her pockets, the late February breeze swirling through her hair. Watching him lean heavily on his cane with each step, she doubted Bruce's idea that he used it only for effect. Then again, she reminded herself, he might be doing exactly that with her.

When he reached her side, he stopped and looked at her, dropping his eyes but keeping his chin lifted in that arrogant way that made prickles run down Maggie's spine. "Figured out where to go so you'll have enough yelling room?" he asked.

Maggie returned his intent, unsmiling look. She felt as if, had she been a cat, every hair on her body would have been standing straight up, every claw unsheathed. She managed to reply coolly, "I was thinking of the old logging road that goes up the mountain at the end of the cul-de-sac. There are some old felled logs we could sit on about a hundred yards uphill, but it's pretty steep."

"I can make it," Galen said, giving her an amused little smile. "Most of my life is spent going uphill one way or another."

"Ah, symbolism," Maggie said, twitching her lips at him in a false smile. She turned away. "Let's go. It'll be getting dark soon."

"Not with that moon up there," Galen said, squinting at the sky. "The air's so clear you can actually see it up here."

It was not air pollution she had come to discuss, so Maggie said nothing. When Galen took hold of her arm she thought of pulling away, but decided against it. She wasn't so thoughtless that she would deny him the support if he needed it, and she didn't want him to think that it bothered her, even though being held in his grasp gave her the uncomfortable feeling he was trying to encompass her in a powerful aura. An aura that would strip away her will and leave her defenseless—an obviously ridiculous notion.

They walked along silently. The bare branches of the winter woods, already deeply shadowed, closed around them, soon cutting them off from the town below as the road curved. Ordinarily, Maggie remembered, going into the hills had made her feel peaceful and serene. This time, every moment of silence added to her building tension. She wondered if she had made a mistake, coming to this remote place with a man who seemed to hate her, but who had commented on her lack of a bra. Perhaps he had cleverly maneuvered her into going to a lonely place with him. The Galen Kendrick she had known would never have harmed her, but this man was someone else altogether. A crashing noise came from the underbrush, and she started and looked at Galen, her heart racing.

"Probably a deer," Galen said, looking amused again. "I don't think there are any muggers up here."

"Very funny." Maggie grimaced and looked quickly away, her heart thumping another notch faster. Darn, but she didn't remember the hill being this steep. Where were those logs, anyway?

"There they are," she said breathlessly a few minutes later, as the small clearing came into view. "I was beginning to wonder if someone had dragged them away."

"I knew they were here," Galen said. "I've come up here several times myself fairly recently."

Doubtless after he'd given her father a sermon on the evils of Balfour Chemicals, Maggie thought. Well, he could just save that story for someone else. She was here to find out what he thought she'd done to deserve his contempt. She brushed futilely at one of the logs, then turned and sat down, wishing she'd changed her clothes, after all. This was no place for a black cashmere coat.

"You should have changed your clothes," Galen said as if he could read her mind. He sat down beside her. "Or is that coat about ready to be discarded?" he asked. "I've seen you wear it twice now."

The strenuous walk had calmed Maggie's anger somewhat, but that remark fueled it instantly, making her so angry she could hear a pulse throbbing in her ears. "No, I thought I could get one more wearing out of it," she snapped. "What business is it of yours, anyway?"

"I was just feeling sympathetic toward the foxes who died to ornament your coat," Galen said, reaching over to fondle the lush blue fox of the collar.

"No, you weren't," Maggie said, slapping his hand away. "You were trying to make me angry, and you've succeeded. What I want to know is why you're being so hateful to me? What do you think I've done that gives you the right to criticize everything about me? You stood there in Beckley looking at me as if I were some contemptible criminal. Did you think I should have recognized you? That I was deliberately snubbing you?"

Galen stared at her, then threw back his head and roared with laughter. "Hell, no," he said. "I knew you didn't recognize me."

"I don't think it's funny," Maggie said, glaring at him. "That leaves no reason at all that I can see."

"No?" Galen put his chin on his hand and leaned toward her. "Try this. You've changed, Maggie. I've seen your pictures. I thought maybe the change I saw was only for the camera, but it isn't. You're phony now, from the top of those kinky curls to the bottom of your dainty feet. I don't like to see someone I used to like and admire change like that."

"You don't know anything about me!" Maggie said loudly. "What makes you think you can take one look at someone and know everything about them?"

"It's much more than one look," Galen said slowly, fixing Maggie with a look so intense that she involuntarily shrank away from him. "It's putting information together. I've heard about your current life-style from your parents. I know you've been seeing Roger Balfour for some time and you've talked of marrying him. I know the kind of money he has, the kind of hypocritical bastard he is. And you'll be just like him someday if you marry him. If you aren't already."

Maggie's eyes narrowed. Inside her pockets, her hands clenched and unclenched. She felt like screaming her response like a shrew, but that was obviously what Galen wanted, for God only knew what perverted reason. With a great effort she managed to say coolly, "A hypocritical bastard? I happen to think Roger is a fine man. He's kind and generous and—" she paused for effect "—a real gentleman."

"You've just proved my point," Galen said in a quiet voice that belied the flashing anger in his eyes. "Up front

he gives to youth organizations and conservation socie-
ties, while out the back door Balfour Chemicals dumps
barrels of toxic waste in a remote area south of their
plant in Charleston. The barrels rust out and the waste
filters into the streams and wells that several thousand
people use for drinking water. They've been forced to
begin cleaning it up, but they're dragging their feet, and
they still haven't paid a cent of the damages won in a series of suits against them. No conclusive proof, they say,
as they make appeal after appeal. Meanwhile, mothers
have buried their children and gone on living there. They
had no money and nowhere else to go.''

This conversation, Maggie thought grimly, was going
exactly where Bruce had warned her it might. Galen
didn't really care a fig whether she was phony or sin-
cere, whether she wore her coat once or a thousand
times. All he cared about was his precious cause. He'd
apparently failed to get the results he wanted through
legal means, and now he was trying to get at Roger Balfour through her. Well, it wasn't going to work! He
wasn't going to trap her into another shouting match.

"That's very sad,'' she said, lifting her chin and
looking at Galen directly, ''but I'm sure that Roger is
doing everything that's legally required while at the same
time looking after the interests of his company. If you're
not getting the results you'd like, perhaps you should
press for additional legislation. I'm sure Roger will
comply with it, also.''

Galen shook his head and sighed. ''You're hard as
nails, aren't you, Maggie? All glitter and no substance.
Whatever became of the lovely girl who helped a crippled, ugly boy, who became his friend when no one else
wanted him around? Who cared about the world, the
children who had nothing when she herself had very lit-

tle? Who cried her eyes out when the baby rabbit she tried so hard to save died? What happened to her, Maggie? Did she die suddenly and you buried her deliberately, or did she just gradually fade away?''

The question hung in the air between them. Maggie tried to stare Galen down, but in the face of the bitter accusation she read in his drawn expression, she found she could not and dropped her gaze. Galen was not playing fair, she thought resentfully. Oh, he was clever, all right, playing first on her anger, then trying for guilt, a guilt she did not deserve. She was not hard as nails. She would still help someone who had no one else to turn to, but in the life she now led she seldom met people who needed anything more than a momentary shoulder to cry on. Now, when she heard of children starving she opened her pocketbook more than most people she knew. She looked at Galen.

"You're wrong, Galen," she said softly. "I'm not any different. I'd still be your friend, even if you looked the same as the last time I saw you. And now when I hear of those children, I still care, only now I can give enough money to make a difference. And I would never give with one hand while taking away with the other."

This time, Galen stared at Maggie for so long that she began to wonder if time had stood still and she only imagined the past years. His eyes glittered strangely in the waning light. Overhead, a gust of wind sent the bare treetops crackling together, then came rushing down the mountainside and whipped through Maggie's hair, sending several strands flying across her face. Before she could brush it back, Galen reached out and did so, then caught one of her earrings in his fingertips and toyed with it. Maggie held very still. The touch of his hand had left a burning trail across her cheek. His fingertips against her earlobe, behind her ear, sent a current through her that made her shiver involuntarily. And still Galen kept looking at her.

"I wonder," he said at last, "if that's really true?" His hand trailed down her throat and parted the fox collar to take hold of the diamond-and-sapphire necklace. "How much did all these jewels cost?" he mused aloud, fingering the necklace and leaning forward to look at it closely. "Perhaps a hundred thousand all together?" He raised his head and looked at Maggie, his eyebrows arched questioningly.

"Something like that," she replied tightly. Having Galen's face so close to hers made her very tense. She wanted to draw back, but was afraid the necklace would break. "Please let go," she said. Galen released the necklace but she still could not move, for he moved his hand behind her neck and threaded his fingers through her hair. She began to feel dizzy, almost frantic. What game was this now? What did Galen want from her?

"Doesn't that bother you?" he asked, massaging the back of her neck with his fingers. "You give a few thousand to UNICEF, or some such organization, and then accept a gift like this? I'm assuming that Roger gave it to you."

"Y-yes," she said shakily, "but that has nothing to do with me. What he spends his money on is his business."

"Oh, I agree," Galen said, cocking his head and looking at her through narrowed eyes. "You buy what you want with your money, and he buys what he wants with his."

Maggie gasped. "Damn you!" she cried, trying to free herself then pushing at Galen with both hands. Instead of letting go, he put his other arm around her. The pale glow of the moon cast deep shadows below his eyes and cheekbones, giving him a sinister look. "Let go of me or I'll scream," Maggie said from between chattering teeth. Galen only pulled her closer.

"What are you so afraid of, Maggie?" he said softly. "Of facing the truth?" With that his mouth descended on hers.

At first Maggie felt nothing but an immense shock wave that shot through her from head to foot and immobilized her like a powerful drug. Then she became aware of an intense heat that emanated to her from Galen's strong, hard body. Everywhere he touched her it pulsed and flared. His lips set her own lips on fire, moving back and forth, suffocating her in a warmth that made her breathless. Her lips parted to gasp for air, and he took advantage to invade and conquer with a sureness that left her trembling and longing for more. The heat within began to melt her limbs. She pressed closer, her arms going around Galen's neck, clutching at him for support. Her hands cooled themselves in the thick, rich silkiness of his hair.

Galen's hand unbuttoned her coat and slipped inside to caress her more intimately, his gentle touch working a magic that made Maggie moan softly at the currents rushing through her and arch to press against his hand. Nothing seemed real. The world was spinning wildly around her. She had Galen's head between her hands, trying to devour his mouth now with her own. When he withdrew his hand and pulled his head back, she stared at him, seeing only his eyes, bright and fierce with passion. He wanted her. It was written there as plainly as if he had said the words. She shuddered, a little frightened, and wondered if her own eyes looked the same, and knew that they must.

"It's a shame all that passion is wasted on Roger Balfour," Galen said, trailing his fingertips along the curve of Maggie's cheek then catching her under the chin. His touch set another flash fire racing through Maggie's trembling body. She watched, fascinated by the soft curve of Galen's lips as he slowly leaned his head down, then closed her eyes as he kissed her lips lingeringly again. She tried to hold him there, but he pulled back and smiled crookedly at her. "That's enough for now. I was afraid maybe I couldn't afford to compete with Roger, but now I'm sure I can." He laughed as Maggie flung him away from her and glared at him.

"I am not for sale to anyone at any price," she snapped. "Roger understands that, and you'd better get it through your head, too."

Galen laughed again, softly. "It was only a figure of speech, Maggie," he said. He looked up. The sky was dark now, a small pattern of stars showing in the gap between the trees that marked the logging road. "We'd better be going before the moon drops behind the mountain." He stood up and held out his hand to her. "Come along."

Maggie frowned at his hand and stood up without touching it. When he took hold of her arm, she shook his hand off and glared at him. Inside she felt as if her mind and body were warring with each other, with her instincts throwing in a few subtle punches for good measure.

"All right, have it your way," Galen said with a shrug, as she moved stiffly into the road and stayed several feet away from him. "I was hoping you'd let me hold on to you."

"You said you'd been up here by yourself," Maggie said. giving him a sideways glance as they started slowly downhill and trying to ignore the surge of guilt that seeing his slow, painful progress caused her. "You must have made it all right then."

"Yes, but it's dark now," Galen replied, "and for some reason, it's harder for me going downhill than up. I don't quite understand the mechanics of it, but that's the way it is."

Was he telling the truth or only trying to play on her sympathies? Maggie wondered. What, exactly, was he up to? She watched him, his head bent as he picked his way along carefully. When he stumbled slightly she grimaced and shook her head, then moved closer to him and held out her arm.

"Thank you," Galen said, giving her a quick smile as he took a firm grip on her arm.

Maggie looked quickly away, but the image of his white teeth flashing against the moon-shadowed darkness of his rugged features stayed with her. Unbidden, the image of the half-crushed face he'd once had, with its ugly scars, replaced it, then faded to his new face. What a beautiful face it was, either way, for those lovely eyes were constant, alive and passionate as no others she had ever seen. A lump came into Maggie's throat. Why, she wondered unhappily, did she feel like crying? What was wrong with her? Was Galen twisting her mind, weaving some kind of spell over her? She didn't need that kind of grief. She had a wonderful life, a beautiful home of her own, and had already resolved to spend more time with her father. What more did she need to do? Whatever problems Roger Balfour had created were not hers to correct. In spite of what Galen might think, she doubted she would have any influence on Roger, anyway, for he kept his business and personal life carefully separated...

At that thought, a little chill ran through Maggie. Could it be that Roger was the hypocrite that Galen thought him, the opportunist that Bruce described? Did the warm, charming man that she knew turn into a vicious monster when he stepped into his other life? No, it wasn't possible. She had known him for almost five years, and there had been no sign.

Galen stumbled a little and leaned heavily on her, then cursed softly. "Sorry," he said, glancing at her and squeezing her arm.

"No problem," Maggie said huskily, for suddenly she wanted nothing so much as to throw her arms around him and hold him close, not out of pity but from sheer admiration for his courage and for all he had accomplished. What had she ever done but take advantage of the looks that nature had given her to make a great deal of money? Then Bruce's words came back to her: "He'll twist your mind. He's a dangerous man." Maggie brushed her windblown hair back with a shaking hand, feeling sick and confused. When they reached the entrance to the cul-de-sac, she had to stifle the impulse to break away from Galen and run back to her parents' house and hide in her room.

The cul-de-sac was bare of cars now, except for a not-so-new looking Buick that Maggie assumed must be Galen's. Even Bruce's shining sports car was gone, and Maggie guessed he had gone home early, probably to see if he could pick up a last-minute date to liven up what had otherwise been a dull weekend for him.

"Are you staying long?" Galen asked as they walked the last little distance to the sidewalk.

"Not very," Maggie replied evasively. She felt Galen stiffen beside her and looked up to catch a flash of anger cross his face. It was just too bad if he didn't like her answer, she thought, her temper flaring. She was not going to spend any more time with him. It was too upsetting, and besides, she was here to spend time with her parents, not let herself in for another round of insults and guilt trips and sexual advances.

When they reached the doorway, Galen took hold of her other arm and jerked her around to face him. "All right, Maggie, tell me how long you're staying. I can find out from your mother, so you might as well tell me in plain and simple English."

Maggie lifted her chin and frowned at him. "Two weeks," she replied, "not that it's any of your business."

"Oh, but it is," Galen said, reaching out to tuck an errant strand of hair from Maggie's face. "I want you to spend a day with me going into the hills and meeting some of the people I've talked about. I think it would increase your understanding of how I feel a million-fold."

"I . . . I won't have time," Maggie said, trying desperately to stand perfectly still and not reveal the way she was trembling at being so close to Galen again and feeling the excitement of his touch. "I want to spend all of my time with my father."

"Coward," Galen said. His eyes narrowed as he studied Maggie's face intently. "What are you afraid of? Me? What Roger might think? Or what you might find out about yourself?"

"I'm not afraid of anything," Maggie said defiantly, although her knees suddenly felt weak as Galen's eyes wandered down to her lips and he smiled that amused little smile again.

"Yes, you are," he said. His smile disappeared abruptly and his expression turned cold. "Either that or

I was treated to a little lapse on your part back there when I kissed you, a sort of emotional slumming. Which was it, I wonder?"

"I don't know what you mean," Maggie said, shaken even more by this sudden switch in Galen's behavior.

"I think you do." Galen let go of Maggie's shoulders and stepped back. "If not, you'd better get it figured out pretty quickly. Time's running out for you, baby. Say good-night to your parents for me." With that, he turned and limped rapidly down the sidewalk. Halfway to the street, he stopped and looked at Maggie, who was staring after him. "If you change your mind, call me," he said, then went toward his car.

Maggie went into the house feeling dazed and emotionally battered.

"Oh, there you are," said her mother, coming into the living room, already wearing a long red bathrobe, her graying hair tucked tidily into a ruffled sleep cap. "I was beginning to think I'd have to send the police to look for you. I just had a bath, but I didn't use up all the hot water. I've already put your father to bed. I'm afraid the day was a little too much for him, but he enjoyed it."

"Yes, I know he did." Maggie nodded. "It . . . the party was a good idea."

"But a lot of work." Her mother sighed. "I think I'll turn in now myself. Did you and Galen have a nice chat?"

"Nice chat?" That was the last thing Maggie would have called it, but she nodded again. "Very . . . nice. He, uh, said for me to tell you good-night."

"He's such a dear," her mother said, smiling. "Watching him grow from that quiet, withdrawn boy he was after the accident to the fine strong man he is now has given your father and me a lot of pleasure. He stops in to see us at least once a month, and calls now and then just to see how we are. It's almost like having a second son." Mrs. Preston tilted her head and frowned at Maggie curiously. "Is something wrong?"

"No, nothing," Maggie said quickly. She had suddenly felt extremely irritated at hearing Galen's praises sung and knew her mother had probably seen her irritation on her face. "I'm tired, too," she said, smiling apologetically. "I think I'll take a bath and go to bed now." She bent and kissed her mother's cheek. "Good night, Mom," she said, giving her a hug. "Sleep well."

Maggie went to her room, hung her coat in the closet, then stood in front of the mirrored dresser to remove her jewelry. She put the earrings carefully into their little box, then unfastened the necklace and stood, holding it in her hand and staring at it. Galen's words echoed in her ears. "You buy what you want with your money, and he buys what he wants with his." Suddenly her hand clenched around the necklace and she turned and flung it as hard as she could across the room. Damn that man! She hated him! Roger had never so much as suggested that she should go to bed with him, after that gift or any of the others he had lavished on her. Not that she would have, even if he had asked. But then, she had never wanted him—not the way she had wanted Galen Kendrick this night. She sat down on the corner of the bed and buried her face in her hands.

"Get hold of yourself, Maggie," she muttered. "It didn't mean anything to Galen. Why should it mean anything to you?"

CHAPTER THREE

IN THE MORNING it was raining, which Maggie thought entirely appropriate for the way she felt. She had tossed and turned all night, waking up so often that she ended up feeling headachy and as tired as if she hadn't slept at all. Nothing made any sense. Not anything Galen said, nor anything he did. Most of all, the way she felt made no sense at all. She felt like some poor, uprooted plant, dangling its bare roots in the air and screaming for the quiet dark and moisture it was used to. The only thing she was sure of was that she did not want to see Galen Kendrick ever again. Roger might not be as exciting, but he had brought a calm orderliness to her life after the first hectic years of her career when she'd had to learn the hard way that some of the jet-set Romeos who suddenly lavished her with attention had only one thing in mind. Let Roger and Galen thrash out their differences in the courts. She would stay well out of it.

"There's my girl," her father said, looking up from the breakfast table and beaming as Maggie came shuffling into the room in her bathrobe and slippers. He held out his arm, and Maggie went to him and gave him a hug and a kiss.

"You're looking chipper this morning," she said, scrutinizing him carefully. His skin was a healthier pink today, the deep lines in his face less pronounced. "I think parties agree with you."

"It wasn't the party," her father said, giving Maggie a loving pat. "It's having the prettiest girl in the world around the house again."

"Such flattery," Maggie chided, pouring herself a cup of coffee from the automatic pot on the counter.

"How do you want your eggs?" her mother asked, standing next to the stove with one in hand, poised to break it into a frying pan.

Ordinarily Maggie didn't eat breakfast and would have argued with her mother over attempts to make her do so, but this morning she didn't feel like arguing. "Over easy," she said, giving her mother a kiss and smiling at her pleased reaction. "Got any aspirin handy?"

"In the cupboard," her mother said, gesturing with the spatula. "Do you have a headache?"

"Just a little one," Maggie replied. "I didn't sleep very well."

"It must seem terribly quiet here after New York," her father commented. "You'll get used to it in a day or two."

"I expect so," Maggie said. She swallowed her aspirin with water then took her coffee and sat down at the table next to her father. "What's on the agenda for today?" she asked. "Recovering from the party?"

"That's about it," he said. "Your mother invited a couple of people who couldn't make it to the party to stop in and visit a while. When we get a day that's not raining, we'll go and drive around some. I like to get out and see how things look, drop in at the miners' café and talk for a while. And we'll drive out and see the Kendricks. They still think the world of you for what you did for Galen years ago, and they made us promise to bring you to see them when you were here."

"Sounds nice," Maggie said, trying to look pleased while at the same time wishing it would rain bucketfuls all the time she was there. Not only did she not want to see Galen, she didn't want to hear about him, either, and Mr. and Mrs. Kendrick were sure to go on and on about their only son.

"By the way," Mrs. Preston said, setting a plate of bacon and eggs and toast in front of Maggie, "Bruce wants you to come and see his new place next Saturday. He said he's planning a little party and he'll let you know the time later."

"I expect he wants to show his place off," Maggie said. "It sounded pretty fancy."

Mrs. Preston sniffed. "Too fancy, if you ask me. I can't figure out how he can have enough money to pay for that and a fancy new car, too."

"Must have good credit," Maggie said over a mouthful of food. She had wondered about the same thing, but had assumed that a man whose business was accounting must know how to keep track of his own money. "Mmm, this is good," she said, munching on a piece of crisp bacon, a fattening luxury she seldom allowed herself. The eggs tasted good too, as well as the whole-wheat toast with homemade apricot preserves. Whatever her emotional state, she was famished, and for a change she was going to indulge herself and not worry about gaining a couple of ounces.

For the rest of that day and the next two, it poured rain. Maggie lazed around the house, playing cribbage and gin rummy with her father, and visiting with the people who stopped by. During the daytimes, she managed to push thoughts of Galen Kendrick to the back of her mind, but at night they crept out to haunt her while she tossed and turned and sleep evaded her.

The more she thought about it, the surer she was that he had deliberately set out to get her off balance. What was his motivation? She toyed briefly with the idea that perhaps her parents had put him up to it in order to break up her relationship with Roger, but decided against it. Her decision about whom to marry was something they would respect. They might not approve, but they would never interfere. The idea that Galen was trying to use her to get to Roger seemed most plausible, but that didn't jibe with the character of a man so devoted to a difficult and sometimes unrewarding cause. But maybe he was desperate enough to try anything.

Most confusing of all was his parting shot that she had better hurry up and decide about her response to him because time was running out for her. What time? Where? Did he think her response was part of some phony bag of tricks she'd learned and tossed to him like a princess throwing a beggar a penny? If only it had been! Her response had been completely spontaneous, and that fact disturbed her more than anything else, for it had left her with a level of unrequited longing that she had never experienced before, a longing that grew worse instead of better as time went by.

If Roger had made her feel that way, they would have been in bed years ago. Married. With a couple of children. Unless, of course, she did not turn Roger on. He told her he adored her, kissed her with enthusiasm, but never attempted anything more than a few innocuous caresses. Could it be that sexually he was not really interested? That what she had taken for strong principles and a noble, gentlemanly character was only a lack of passion, that very lack permitting him to do what both

Bruce and Galen had told her he did—go after what he wanted using any means that worked?

"That would be a fine kettle of fish," Maggie muttered, sitting up in bed Tuesday night and rubbing her throbbing forehead. She tried to feel betrayed and unhappy that Roger might have fooled her but could muster no more than a small annoyance. Her thoughts returned almost immediately to Galen. There was no lack of passion there. He had shaken her to her very core, made her furious, and at the moment there was no idea more appealing to her than getting Galen alone on one of those tiny deserted Fijian islands and making passionate love day and night. Was she ever confused!

Maggie flopped onto her stomach and pulled the covers over her head. She had to stop thinking and get some sleep, or she was going to look like a wreck in the morning. The weather had cleared late that day. March was going to come in like a lamb. And her mother had called the Kendricks and arranged to stop by and see them the next afternoon.

It was ten o'clock in the morning by the time Maggie scuffed her bleary-eyed way into the kitchen to be greeted by her mother's cheery, "Good morning, sleepyhead. It's a beautiful day. Remember, we're going to go and visit the Kendricks this afternoon."

Maggie nodded. "I remember." She poured herself a cup of coffee and sank into a chair, staring morosely out at the sunny yard. She was a mess. Life was a mess. What business did the sun have shining so brightly?

"How about some pancakes this morning?" her mother suggested.

"Lovely," Maggie agreed. What difference did it make if she got fat? She could model queen-size clothes.

"I'm glad to see you're not starving yourself like you did the last time you were here," her father commented, smiling at her approvingly. "If you don't have your health, you have nothing."

Her father's words jolted Maggie out of her self-indulgent misery. How foolish and ungrateful she was, fretting about her own minor problems. Impulsively she put her hand over his. "Have I told you this morning that I love you?" she said huskily.

"I love you, too," her father said, putting his other hand on top of hers and blinking rapidly at the same time as he smiled. "Lord, how I wish..." he began, then stopped and shook his head and gave Maggie's hand a squeeze. "I'm just glad you're here," he finished.

"Me, too," Maggie said, knowing very well what he wished. He wished she could be here, or at least closer, all the time. But there was no work for her here, and if she married Roger... Maggie pushed that thought from her mind. She was going to take things one day at a time for a while. And today she had to cope with visiting the Kendricks.

When her father awakened from his after-lunch nap they all piled into her parents' roomy old Chrysler and started for the Kendricks', with Maggie driving. Maggie had put on beige whipcord slacks, a rust-colored sweater and a beige Windbreaker, along with her sturdy walking shoes, in spite of her mother's not very subtle hints that she should be more dressed up.

"You know Mrs. Kendrick will want to show me the stables," Maggie said, "and I'd feel like a fool wobbling around in high heels." She knew that her mother's concern was not only for having Maggie looking her model best. Even though the Kendricks were not standoffish, they were held in awed respect by the rest of the town. The source of their apparent fortune was something of a mystery, Mr. Kendrick's ownership of the local bank not a sufficient explanation. Some thought that Mrs. Kendrick had inherited a large sum from her family, others that Mr. Kendrick had a dark and excitingly profitable past. Whatever the source, the beautiful horse farm, Haven Hill, which took up most of the northern end of the valley beyond Spring Mountain, was a source of local pride, inevitably pointed out to visiting friends and relatives.

As soon as Maggie turned the car off the road and down the lane that led to the Kendricks' house, she felt a sense of nostalgia so overwhelming that tears sprang to her eyes. On either side of the lane were huge pastures, surrounded by sturdy white board fences. On the right, several mares, round-sided and close to foaling, were grazing. It was here that Maggie had first come to read to Galen, taken her first terrified ride on a horse, seen for the first time the birth of a foal.

"It still looks the same," she said. "I've always thought they should make a movie here, it's so perfect."

"Sheila Kendrick works mighty hard to keep it that way," said Mrs. Preston. "She has a lot of help, but there's no job too tough for her to tackle. She's a very determined lady."

"I know," Maggie said. The huge Victorian house with its gingerbread trim, corner tower and wide veranda in the grove of oak trees that they now approached was testimony to that fact. The house had once been on a corner lot in Spring Mountain. It had been exactly what Mrs. Kendrick had always wanted, so she had bought it and had it moved the three miles to the spot where she wanted it, blithely ignoring warnings that it couldn't be done.

When Maggie stopped the car in the wide circular drive in front of the house, both Mr. and Mrs. Kendrick came out to greet them.

"Maggie, dear, how wonderful to see you," Sheila Kendrick said, coming toward her with her hands outstretched. "We're so proud of you, but we've missed you terribly. We really have."

Maggie bent and accepted kisses on both her cheeks from the tiny woman with silver-blond hair, noticing that she still looked every bit the Virginian aristocrat, in spite of the lines that years in the out-of-doors had given her delicate features. She also still dressed in jodhpurs and riding boots, always ready for a ride on one of the champion hunters that she raised. In all the times Maggie had seen her, she could only remember seeing her in a dress once or twice.

"You're the pride and joy of Spring Mountain," said Mr. Kendrick, giving Maggie a massive embrace. Galen's father was a huge, hearty man, from whom Galen got his dark coloring and height. When Maggie was younger, she had thought that he looked like a bear. Now he seemed to her to epitomize an eighteenth-century squire, a man used to enjoying the good things of life while he ruled his estate with a fair but iron hand.

"There's that boy now," said Mrs. Kendrick, the happy lilt of her voice interrupting Maggie's exchange of pleasantries with her husband. "He said he'd be here for lunch. He's only two hours late."

That boy? Maggie's heart lurched violently and started racing. She turned her head, following Mrs. Kendrick's eyes. That boy's car was rapidly coming up the lane.

As the car drew nearer, Maggie stared at it numbly, rooted to the spot, while waves of dizziness washed over her. She could not have moved if she'd wanted to. She thought wildly that it was like one of those dreams where you tried to run away from some fearsome pursuer and could neither move nor scream.

Galen brought his car to a stop, got slowly out of it, then turned to greet them. "Hello, everyone," he said, sweeping the group with his eyes and smiling. "Sorry I'm late," he said to his mother, bending to kiss her cheek. "I got hung up on the telephone and I picked up a hamburger on the way, so you don't need to think I'm starving." Then he turned to Maggie. "Hello, Maggie," he said gravely. "Have you been enjoying your vacation?"

Maggie suddenly realized that both her jaw and hands were tightly clenched and she was staring wide-eyed at Galen, drinking in his appearance as a parched sponge would water. He was wearing a white turtleneck sweater, boots and tight black riding pants, and the sight of him made her want to touch him so much her fingers tingled. She took a deep breath before she spoke, afraid her voice would come out like a croak, if it came at all. "Yes, I have," she finally replied. "It's been very restful."

"Maybe a little too restful," Maggie's father put in. "Spring Mountain's pretty dull after New York City."

"Well, I've got an antidote for that," Mrs. Kendrick said, smiling first at Maggie and then at Galen. "I'm going to send these two young people off on a ride. I'll bet Maggie doesn't get to ride much anymore, and Galen doesn't come to exercise his horse nearly often enough. I told Galen he had to do that today. That's why he's wearing his riding clothes."

"Oh, I couldn't," Maggie began, then closed her mouth. Galen's eyes were crinkling into an amused smile. Whether she had been neatly set up she wasn't sure, but she did know that arguing with Mrs. Kendrick was as useless as talking to the moon. If only she'd taken her mother's advice and worn a dress, she thought. But that might not have helped. Sheila Kendrick doubtless kept a supply of riding habits in all sizes.

"Henry, you take the Prestons into the house while I introduce Maggie to my little mare," Mrs. Kendrick said to her husband. "I'll be back in a jiffy."

They walked toward the green-painted stables, which were set a short distance behind the house in a network of paddocks, Mrs. Kendrick chattering happily about her horses. Maggie scarcely heard a word she said, she was so aware of Galen, swinging along beside her. She finally came back to dazed reality when they reached the stables and Galen went to get his horse and saddle it. Mrs. Kendrick put a bridle on a pretty chestnut mare with a white blaze on its forehead and led her out for Maggie.

"This is my jewel," said Mrs. Kendrick. "Her name is Valentine, but I call her Val. See the shape of that blaze?"

"It is sort of heart-shaped, isn't it?" Maggie said, taking another deep breath and swallowing hard. "I'm afraid it's been a very long time since I've ridden."

"Val's as gentle as a lamb," Mrs. Kendrick assured her. "Galen will give you a little refresher course if you've forgotten anything. Here, just lead her down toward the tack room. He'll help you saddle her. I'll get back to my other guests." She handed the reins to Maggie. "See you later," she said brightly.

Maggie nodded, took yet another deep breath and started down the stables in the direction of Galen. She had gone only a few steps when Galen finished saddling his big bay gelding and turned to watch her. She was so conscious of his eyes on her that for the first time since her earliest days as a model, she had the terrible feeling that her feet did not belong to her and might become entangled at any moment. Telling herself not to be an idiot did no good. She *was* one, and there seemed no help for it. The only thing that remained would be for Galen to start attacking her again for her shortcomings now that they were alone. If he did, she would probably fall in a blubbering heap at his feet.

To her relief, Galen seemed to have adopted an entirely different strategy this day, perhaps because he was at his parents' home and she was technically his guest. "Need some help saddling her?" he asked quietly when she drew near.

"I don't remember a thing about it," Maggie replied in a thin little voice. "It's been a long time."

"It has," Galen agreed. "We were never able to ride together, were we?"

"No, we weren't." In Maggie's mind's eye she suddenly pictured Galen, watching from his wheelchair, while his mother taught her the rudiments of riding. "I'm so glad you can ride again," she said.

"So am I." Galen studied Maggie soberly for several moments, then smiled. "So am I," he repeated. "I'll get your saddle."

Maggie stood, clutching the reins, her heart pounding. Dear God, she thought desperately, she had better get hold of herself. She had never known that pure sexual attraction could be this powerful, and it had her completely unnerved. Maybe if she got moving it would help. "Let me try. You tell me what to do," she said when Galen returned and tossed a blanket onto Val's back, followed by the saddle. Galen nodded, and while he gave instructions she did as he told her, praying he would not notice that her hands were shaking.

"Why are you so nervous?" he asked, shattering her hopes that he had not. "Have you become afraid of riding?"

"A little," Maggie replied, thankful for the excuse. "I'll be all right once we get going," she added when Galen frowned.

They led the horses through the paddock. "I had to convince this fellow to let me mount from the right," Galen said as he swung into the saddle. "I didn't think he'd mind, but the first time I tried it he jumped sideways about three feet and I landed on my backside."

"I never thought about that problem," Maggie said, managing to mount Val without having a similar disaster.

"Where to?" Galen asked, looking over at her.

"You lead the way," Maggie said, shrugging. "Just remember that my riding's very rusty."

Galen nodded. "We'll take a few turns around the ring so I can check you out, and then we'll take a trail ride into the hills."

"Fine," Maggie said, trying to smile and keep her voice pleasant and calm. She felt more like screaming to let off some of her tension. And it sounded as if Galen had a long ride planned.

While Maggie took several turns around the riding ring, Galen watched and corrected her. She found that it came back to her very quickly, and the balmy breeze blowing through her hair and cooling her heated face felt heavenly. She unzipped her jacket and let the air caress her moist skin through the weave of her sweater. She had never realized before that physical desire could make a person feel as if they were on a griddle.

"I think you've got it," Galen said when she had cantered around the ring twice, successfully changing leads when he commanded. When she pulled up beside him, he said, "Let's ride up to Bald Knob. I haven't been there in ages."

"All right," Maggie agreed. At least it wasn't the longest trail he could have chosen, nor the steepest.

The trail led from a road close to the north end of the Kendrick property, winding in a series of gentle switchbacks up the thickly wooded side of a mountain, then following the steep nose of a ravine to a cleared space at the top. A gnarled old cedar stood guard over a small brook that bubbled from a moss-covered crevice in the rocky ground. Along the way, Galen commented on the trees, a rabbit that bounded across their path and an owl that swooped silently off a branch not far overhead and startled his horse.

Maggie replied in short, monosyllabic statements, quite aware that she sounded like a fool but unable to do any better. She was riding behind Galen; watching his thick black hair blowing in the wind and his broad shoulders and trim hips had her in such a state that she was within an inch of turning poor Val around and galloping off in the opposite direction. Only her pride and a stubborn determination to overcome this idiocy prevented it.

When they reached the summit, Galen drew his horse to a stop and dismounted. "Let's take a breather and give the horses a rest, too," he said. "They can get a drink from the stream." He led his horse close to it and dropped the reins.

After she had dismounted, Maggie led Val to the little creek, standing beside her and holding her reins loosely. From the corner of her eye she had seen Galen limp the short distance to the top, where he leaned against the old cedar tree. She also knew that he probably expected her to join him and was not surprised when he called to her.

"Let her go and come up here," he said. "There's a beautiful view. She's not going anywhere."

"I, uh, all right," Maggie said. She dropped the reins and started toward Galen. It could not have been more than thirty feet, but it seemed like a mile. This was ridiculous, she told herself. Galen had lured her up here. It had all been a plot. She should be furious. She wasn't. She tried to look away toward the valley, but stumbled and had to catch herself and brush the pebbles from her stinging hands.

"Are you all right?" Galen asked.

"Fine," Maggie lied. "Just fine." She stopped about five feet from Galen and deliberately turned to look at the valley below. All she saw were shimmering streaks of color and light and shade. She blinked, took a deep breath and clenched her hands together. At the sound of Galen's voice she started as if she had been shot and turned her head to look at him.

"What's bothering you, Maggie?" he asked. "You're all tied up in knots."

"Nothing in particular," she replied, shrugging and trying to smile. "It's just one of those days. I'm a little on edge for no particular reason."

Galen smiled. This time, Maggie noticed, he did not look amused. It was a nice smile, and his eyes were glowing with a soft warmth, not mocking. He beckoned with one forefinger. "Come here, Maggie," he said softly. "I know what the problem is."

"Y-you do?" Maggie stammered while her feet moved her toward him without asking her if she wanted them to, the light in his eyes drawing her like a beacon.

"Uh-huh," he said, still smiling. When she was within arm's reach, he took her hand and pulled her close to him. His other hand threaded through her hair and tucked behind her neck, while his eyes scanned her face and rested lingeringly on her lips.

Maggie stood motionless, mesmerized, devouring the strong face before her hungrily with her eyes, her breathing shallow, her lips parted. Her lips felt swollen, hungry for the touch of Galen's mouth on hers. She could feel the heat and hardness of his body as his arm slid behind her and pressed her against him, and her own tense body responded with shooting fires of longing so intense she thought she might explode if Galen did not kiss her soon. While time stood still, he stared at her, and Maggie was sure that in his eyes she saw a mirror of her own longing. Briefly a shadow of some inner conflict crossed his face, then, with a groan, he lowered his mouth to hers.

An explosion of sensations rocketed through Maggie, leaving her limp and shaken. She felt as if the top of the mountain must have erupted like a volcano and sent them flying together into space. Galen's mouth was punishing, demanding against hers, but no more so than her response. She flung her arms around his neck and clung to him, plunging one hand into the thick black hair at his nape, moving her fingers to take in yet another delicious sensation. A hypnotic scent filled her nostrils, pungent and musky, a blend of Galen and cedar, sunshine and horses. The touch of his cool fingers creeping beneath her sweater made her tremble in anticipation.

Slowly they sank together to the ground. With one hand Galen cradled Maggie's head, protecting it from the harsh ground, while with the other he pushed her sweater up. His lips trailed slowly down her chin and neck. His hand rested across her slender rib cage, warm and rough and strong, while his kisses lingered on her throat, then wandered upward to tease behind her ears. In a daze of desire, Maggie moved restlessly beneath his hand, wild fantasies of what might be about to happen flying through her mind. With some surprise, she registered the fact that she wouldn't mind at all. If Galen were to take off her sweater, she would shamelessly help him do it. But instead, Galen slowly pulled down her sweater and raised himself on one elbow beside her, smiling and kissing her lips again and again.

"Heavenly, isn't it?" he murmured, pressing his cheek to hers, then smiling at her again.

"Yes," she answered hoarsely. And it could be even more heavenly, if only... She pushed the thought away, trying to ignore the empty ache that racked her, reading in Galen's eyes that he would go no further. She had all but given him an invitation. No other man had been able to destroy her defenses like that. Why had he stopped? He played with a strand of her hair, and she could see thoughts flitting through his mind behind the clear gray of his eyes. "What are you thinking?" she asked.

"Many things," he answered soberly. He abruptly sat back, then got to his feet and held out his hand to help Maggie up. When she stood before him, he cradled her face between his hands and kissed her lightly. "Do you suppose now," he asked, "that I could persuade you to spend a day with me next week?"

Maggie stiffened, feeling as if ice water had been suddenly thrown in her face. She pulled away from Galen, frowning, her hands clenched at her sides. Now she understood what Galen had meant when he said that he could compete with Roger Balfour. He could get what he wanted by using her response to him!

"Is this what you meant by buying what you want?" she demanded.

"Maggie," Galen said, his face darkening, "don't be so damned literal."

"Literal?" she snapped. "I'm not being literal. You lured me up here and then used the fact that I was so stupidly transparent about wanting you to kiss me to try and get what you wanted, didn't you? Well, it isn't going to work, and I'll be damned if I ever let you kiss me or touch me again, so you don't need to go planning any more of these little escapades!"

With that, Maggie whirled and started toward her horse, angrily thinking that next time he probably would try to go all the way in hopes that would persuade her. What a gullible fool she was!

"Don't be a damned fool, Maggie," Galen yelled after her, but she ignored him, flung herself onto Val's back, wheeled around and started down the trail before Galen was even in his saddle, breathing hard and cursing herself under her breath. She should have known. How stupid could she be? That was the last time her rampaging hormones would take over like that! The very last!

When they arrived at the stables, the bristling hostility between them was so thick that it could have been cut with a knife. Wordlessly Maggie put away Val's tack and led her to her stall. She had started toward the door when she felt Galen's hand close over her shoulder like a vise.

"Let go of me!" she snarled, turning to glare at him.

"No," he replied, fixing her with an intent, penetrating glare of his own. "You're a fool, Maggie," he said. "Either that or you're more completely beyond hope than I thought. Which is it?"

"I don't know what you're talking about," Maggie said, "and I don't care! Let go!" She tried futilely to shake off his hand. "Do you want me to scream?"

"No, I want you to listen to me," Galen replied, his face stony. "I don't believe you're really beyond hope, maybe only because I don't want to. But I do know that your mind is going in two directions while your heart can only go in one. Choose the wrong path, and it will surely die. You might pay attention to your body. It's trying to tell you something."

So saying, he crushed her against him, covering her mouth with his in a kiss that was so punishing yet passionate that all Maggie's efforts to blank out the sensations she felt were useless. She stood still, trembling, with tears in her eyes when he released her, the fire in his eyes in stark contrast to his still stony face.

"Now," he said gruffly, "I suggest we both make an attempt to look reasonably normal for our parents' sake. After all, we have just been for a pleasant ride up the mountain, haven't we?" He cocked a sardonic eyebrow at Maggie, then went to the door and held it open for her. "After you," he said in mockingly deferential tones.

The rest of the afternoon went whirling by like a nightmare. Maggie knew that she must be succeeding in doing as Galen had suggested, for she could hear herself laughing and feel her lips smiling, but they seemed to belong to someone else. She tried not to look at Galen, but now and then her eyes strayed to meet his. Each time, the impact of his intense gaze made her hands clench around the arms of the chair where she sat. She could have screamed in relief when her mother refused the Kendricks' invitation to stay for dinner, saying that her father was not up to such a long time away from home.

"Do come back real soon, Maggie," Sheila Kendrick said in her warm Southern drawl.

"I will," Maggie promised, avoiding Galen's eyes as he held the door of the car open for her.

She got in, and could not avoid looking at him when he bent and said softly, "Call me if you change your mind." She opened her mouth to say she'd be damned if she would, then closed it, ignoring the amused smile that played around Galen's lips as he closed the door and gave her a little farewell salute.

"The Kendricks are the dearest people," Maggie's mother said as they drove away. "Of all the people I've ever met, I think I admire and envy Sheila Kendrick more than anyone, and it's not because of the money she has. She's so sparkling and alive, it's a tonic to be with her."

"I understand what you mean," said Mr. Preston. "She's a happy woman. She loves her home, her husband, her horses and her son. What more could any woman want?"

What more, indeed? Maggie thought bitterly. Mrs. Kendrick had her life all wrapped up in a tidy little package. Why couldn't her own life fall neatly into place like that?

CHAPTER FOUR

"Is SOMETHING bothering you?" Maggie's father asked the next day, when Maggie stared blankly into space instead of making her move on the cribbage board. "You seem a million miles away."

"No, just wool-gathering," Maggie said, grimly returning her attention to the game. "Let's see, where was I?"

Her father put his cards down. "I don't think you feel like playing. Are you missing Roger?"

"No!" Maggie spoke so vehemently that her father raised his eyebrows in surprise, and she immediately felt guilty. "I mean, I do miss him, but that wasn't what I was thinking about," she said.

"What, then?" her father persisted. "Since yesterday you've been as edgy as a treed coon. Did you and Galen have a fight? The air was pretty thick with something when you two came back from that ride."

"We had a bit of a disagreement," Maggie said tightly. "I'd rather not talk about it." She didn't want to think about it, either, but she couldn't seem to stop. For five minutes she would think that she'd been perfectly justified for being so angry with Galen, and for the next five she would feel equally strongly that she'd been stupid. Why not spend the day with him? What was she so afraid of? Of learning that Galen was right, that Roger really was a hypocrite, or...something else?

She felt no better the next day, but by the time she began to get ready for Bruce's party, she had managed to generate a seething anger against Galen. What right did he have coming into her life and picking it apart, throwing her emotions into a tailspin? Whether Galen thought so or not, she cared about the people who could have been poisoned by Balfour Chemicals' thoughtless dumping of toxic wastes, and she intended to speak to Roger about it. Galen had accomplished his purpose, so forget him and his attempt to seduce her into seeing the tragedy firsthand. She didn't need it. What she needed was a diversion, a party with bright, interesting people and witty conversation.

Preparing to put on her makeup, Maggie leaned over the washbasin and peered into the bathroom mirror, pinching her rounded cheeks together with one hand. Great, just great. To top it all off she was gaining weight, and some damned photographer was sure to tell her she looked like a fat pig. A fat pig at five foot nine, one hundred and twenty pounds. It wasn't her fault that when she was upset she ate. Other people might lose their appetite, but not her. She became ravenous.

Maggie picked her wet washcloth from the basin and dabbed hopefully at a smudge beneath her eye, hoping that it was smeared makeup and would wash off. It wasn't. She knew it wouldn't be. She was getting dark shadows from lack of sleep.

"I should have stayed in New York," she muttered. Then none of this would ever have happened. Wouldn't that have been wonderful? She frowned at the washcloth, then wadded it up and threw it across the room, where it hit the pink-tiled wall with a soggy thud. No, it wouldn't have been wonderful! Her father needed her. He needed to see her and touch her and feel her love again. Nothing in the world was any more important than that, especially since she had begun to suspect that her parents were worried about Bruce and more than a little upset with his new attitude and life-style. Oh, they smiled and said how proud they were of him, but she could tell. They would have much preferred that he be more like Galen.

Galen again. Maggie scowled darkly at her reflection. The man had gotten under her skin like a tropical parasite. Well, he could just get out of it. "Too bad Roger can't be here, too," Bruce had said. She was glad he wasn't. She was angry with him, too. The least he could have done was call her. Just because he was in China didn't mean he should neglect her. That was his way, though. He was often gone for long periods on business, seldom bothering to call. Too busy. Then he tried to make up for it when he was home, showering her with gifts and attention. She wasn't sure she liked that.

Theirs had been, Maggie mused as she smoothed on her makeup base, a rather strange relationship from the beginning. At first they had dated occasionally, then, for the past two years, more frequently, although with both their busy schedules that was usually only one week out of a month, sometimes less often. Still, there became a sort of tacit agreement between them that they were drifting toward something permanent. Maggie had been quite sure that Roger was the right man for her, until . . .

Maggie picked up the washcloth and wrung it out viciously. Galen. Drat the man! He had made her doubt both Roger and herself.

"Maggie, are you ready?" came her mother's voice from the hallway. "It's almost time for you to leave for Bruce's."

"I can tell time, Mother," Maggie replied sharply, glancing at her watch. Yes, it was almost time to leave, but it would only take her a few more minutes to get ready. She quickly put on her makeup, then a short black satin cocktail dress with a silver sequined jacket and black patent sandals with very high heels. In them she towered over most men, but she was used to that. Even Roger was barely her height when she wore them. Of course, Galen...

Maggie cursed under her breath to squelch the rest of that thought and put on her opossum fur jacket, surveying the total result with satisfaction. It was a good thing she had brought one dressy outfit. She knew Bruce would never have forgiven her if she didn't dress to the hilt to impress his friends, a role she did not particularly like. It made her feel like some kind of specimen on display. It was one thing to be gawked at as a professional, but quite another in her personal life.

Maggie's father gave a long, low whistle when he saw her. "Spectacular," he said, laughing when Maggie stuck out her tongue at him. She kissed her parents goodbye, listened patiently while her father warned her not to drive too fast in that old car with those old tires, then left, after telling them not to wait up for her.

The road wound through the mountains, the snow all washed away by the rain, the grass beginning to show green on the southern slopes. Bruce's party was not scheduled to begin until eight, but he had asked Maggie to come early so that he could show her around his apartment and they could have a light supper before the guests arrived.

"I'd be glad to help you get ready," Maggie had offered, but Bruce had assured her he needed no help. He was having the event catered.

Once she reached the interstate, the drive was less than an hour, and Maggie followed the directions Bruce had given her through an older part of Charleston with big square two-story houses, past a new little shopping center to an elegantly landscaped entrance gate with a large brass sign that proclaimed Deer Creek Manor.

"Pretty pretentious," Maggie said to herself as she turned down the drive between the rows of starkly modern buildings, with their cantilevered balconies and huge expanses of glass set off by walls of angled siding. She found Bruce's building and parked between two BMWs. Welcome to yuppieville, Maggie thought with a grimace.

Bruce opened the door before she could knock. "Wow! Do you look gorgeous," he said, grinning appreciatively. "Welcome to my humble abode. Boy, is this going to be something, having you here. Let me take your coat." He hung Maggie's jacket in a closet with mirrored doors, while Maggie looked around the dramatic room, amazed.

"You must have hired a decorator," she commented. "This is really lovely, Bruce."

"Thanks. Yes, I did have a decorator. Best in Charleston, to be exact. I couldn't tackle anything like this myself." He took Maggie's arm. "Let me show you around." He led Maggie through the entire apartment, beaming at her approving comments about the charming little dining room, the two sumptuous bedrooms, the elaborate baths. They ended up in the kitchen, where a young woman in a white uniform was putting the finishing touches on a tray of hors d'oeuvres and another was stirring something on the range.

"That looks delicious," Maggie said, eyeing the elegant stuffed mushrooms and tiny shrimp canapés hungrily.

"Nothing but the best for my beautiful sister," Bruce said, opening the refrigerator and taking out a bottle of expensive champagne. "I thought we'd start out with a little toast, then have some dinner. Shall we go into the dining room?"

"Why not?" Maggie said. If she'd had doubts about Bruce's pocketbook matching his expensive taste before, she now had serious questions about his sanity. From what she had seen, there was no way he could afford all this. A millionaire would be doing well to have acquired some of the expensive special touches the decorator had provided—Leroy Neimann prints, cordovan leather upholstery, custom-built wall units.

At the table, Bruce opened the champagne then poured it into Waterford crystal flutes. "To us," he said, raising his glass. "May our future continue to be prosperous."

Maggie looked at him thoughtfully. "May I add something? Let's put in a hope that we keep our health. Dad reminded me, without intending to, that without health, nothing else matters very much."

"A good, but sobering, thought," Bruce agreed with a grin as he clinked his glass against Maggie's then took a drink of his champagne. "I really admire you, sticking it out for two weeks with Mom and Dad. It must be pretty dull for you."

"I haven't found it dull," Maggie said, thinking wryly that dull would have been a lot more restful. "In fact it makes me feel good to be able to make Dad happy. I plan to come home a lot more often from now on."

"Really?" Bruce looked surprised, then his eyes narrowed. "That wouldn't have anything to do with Galen Kendrick, would it?"

Startled, Maggie could only stare at her brother for a moment before she answered, "Why would you say such a thing? You know our father's ill. I want to spend more time with him while I can."

"Yeah," Bruce said, still eyeing Maggie suspiciously, "but I saw the way Kendrick looked at you last Sunday. I didn't like it one bit. And I was going to mention to you that it would be a good idea if you passed the word along to Mom and Dad not to have Galen hanging around there so much. It doesn't look good, and I know Roger Balfour wouldn't go for it."

While Bruce had been speaking, Maggie had first been amazed, then appalled. By the time he finished she was so angry that the top of her head throbbed as if it were about to explode. "How dare you suggest such a thing?" she snapped. "Our parents can have anyone they want to come to their house, and if I feel like seeing Galen, I will. He's one of the finest men I've ever met."

"I was afraid he'd get to you," Bruce said, his lip curling in disgust. "Boy, he's a fast worker. He's nothing but a rabble-rouser, Maggie. Here's poor Roger, trying his best to fix up a bad situation, and Kendrick does nothing but make trouble for him." He leaned forward and gave Maggie an earnest look. "That's bound to hurt the feelings of a sensitive man like Roger Balfour, don't you think?"

"I never thought of it that way," Maggie said, frowning. Something about Bruce's earnest plea didn't make sense. At her parents' party, he had suggested that Roger might not be upset if she used her wiles on Galen, which was about as insensitive as a man could get. Now, since she hadn't liked his first suggestion, he was taking another tack. Bruce was getting pretty shifty and opportunistic, and she didn't like what that implied about his character. . . .

"Well, you should," Bruce said, looking smugly triumphant. "Roger really worries about things like that."

Maggie took a sip of her champagne and stared at Bruce thoughtfully. If Roger did, she had never heard about it. In fact, Roger had never said one word about the whole business with Galen Kendrick. Still, both of them left their work behind when they met, their time together devoted to more esoteric and entertaining pastimes. She had liked it that way. Now she didn't, thanks to Galen and his blasted meddling. Bruce was right, he was a fast worker. But Bruce himself had made her wonder just how well she really knew Roger Balfour. Why did Bruce seem to know so much?

"You and Roger seem to have gotten very well acquainted," she commented. "Much better than I knew."

Bruce shrugged. "He's a real tiger when it comes to finances, so naturally he's always interested in the balance sheets. We have a session every time he comes to the plant."

"How often is that?" Maggie asked.

"Every other month," Bruce replied. He grinned suddenly. "Let's talk about something else. Business gets boring. Seen any good plays lately?"

At that point, one of the caterer's helpers interrupted with the first course of dinner, which left Maggie a few minutes to speculate about Bruce's relationship with Roger. She had an unpleasant feeling about it. Bruce had changed, not for the better, and Roger was somehow involved. She also had the impression that Bruce was hiding something. Probably just her imagination, she decided, but still, the suspicion did not go away.

The dinner of broiled lamb chops was delicious, the conversation general, with no more references to either Roger or Galen. Promptly at eight the party guests began to arrive, giving Maggie such awed and deferential treatment she remarked to Bruce that she felt like something from the wax museum. They were all young professional and business couples, most of them two-income families whose chief topics of conversation were their recent acquisitions of cars, boats and other paraphernalia of the good life.

Maggie made conversation with the guests, but found that she had little in common with them. They were still scrambling for success, with worries that she had rocketed past in only a few years' time. It made her feel uncomfortable, but she knew that her smiles and intelligent remarks covered her discomfort, and no one guessed that she was bored, often finding herself wishing that she was home in old comfortable clothes with a good book to read. It was, she mused wryly, an educational evening, a glimpse into another part of life that she had read about but barely experienced. Bruce seemed oblivious to the difference, delighted at her ability to charm his friends.

By the time midnight approached, Maggie's head was aching and she was feeling almost claustrophobic, trapped in a room full of people she could not smile at or talk to for one more minute. Desperate to get away, she fell back on a tried and true excuse to take her leave.

"Don't tell anyone," she whispered to Bruce, "but my feet are killing me. I've loved your party. Let's get together for dinner next week, on me." At that time, she hoped to lead him to discuss some of the things that were worrying her.

Bruce hugged Maggie tightly as he helped her into her jacket. "It's been great," he said huskily. "I'm sure glad you're planning to come home more often. I've missed you. We used to be so darn close."

"We'll fix that," Maggie promised, more certain than ever that something was bothering her brother. "I'll call you tomorrow."

She went outside and got into her parents' old car, now sandwiched between a Corvette and a Porsche, and started to trace her path toward home. Her head was really throbbing. Instead of cheering her up, Bruce's party had made her feel worse. She was worried about him and no less confused about herself. Why on earth couldn't she have relaxed and had a good time at a party with a nice group of people her own age? Maybe if Bruce hadn't made that stupid suggestion about Galen... Now where was the cross street? Oh, yes, after the shopping center.

She passed the new shopping center, deserted and dimly lit, and turned down the street through the sedate older part of town. She had gone only a few blocks when the steering suddenly began pulling hard toward the right. "Oh, Lord," Maggie groaned, her heart sinking, "I've got a flat." She pulled the car over next to the curb and stopped. An inspection proved her right. The right front tire was almost completely flat.

"What do I do now?" Maggie said aloud, pushing her hair from her aching forehead and looking around. She was on a quiet residential street, far from any telephone booth, and the houses nearby were dark, their occupants already in bed for the night. Traffic was nonexistent. There would doubtless be a public telephone at the shopping center, but it was blocks away, close to a mile. In these damned high heels, she'd be crippled by the time she got there. Still, what else could she do? She might as well start to walk. On the way, she might be able to flag down a passing car. If she saw a house with lights on, she'd knock on the door. This wasn't New York. People here were friendly toward their fellow humans in dire straits.

A block down the street, Maggie saw a car approaching. She was about to step to the curb and wave when a horrible thought struck her. In her present attire, she did not look terribly respectable by West Virginian standards. What if the car was inhabited by a group of men? Instead of waving, she thrust her hands into her pockets and strode along, her chin in the air. She crossed one street, walked another block and stopped at the second cross street, her feet crying out for a rest. Leaning against a lamp post, she looked up and down the cross street. Two doors to her left, lights gleamed from a second-story window. Someone was still up, she thought, or they slept with their lights on. It was worth a try. She walked down the street to the house, opened the gate into a fenced yard and started up the sidewalk. She had only gone a few steps when a large black dog came racing toward her, barking furiously.

"Help!" Maggie screamed loudly as she jumped sideways, lost her balance and fell, still screaming. Seconds later, the dog was on top of her but, instead of biting her, it began to lick her face.

Meanwhile, the porch lights came on, a door flew open and a deep male voice commanded, "Get back, Betsy!" The dog stopped licking and trotted away. Un-

even footsteps came toward her. Maggie raised her head.
Her heart almost stopped beating.

"Galen!" she cried. "Is that you?"

CHAPTER FIVE

"MAGGIE! MY GOD, what are you doing here this time of night? Are you all right?" Galen said. He leaned down and pulled her to her feet, while the dog came back, wagging her tail hopefully.

"I'm okay, I think. I...I had a flat tire a few blocks away," Maggie gasped, her heart pounding as she clutched at Galen's arm and struggled to pull her sandals on. "I was looking...your dog scared me...for someplace to call for help, and your light was on."

"And you didn't even know where I lived," Galen said flatly.

Maggie looked up at him. "No."

Galen cocked an eyebrow and smiled a wry little half smile. "I should have guessed from the way you're dressed that you didn't come to see me. Must have been one of Bruce's soirees."

"Yes," Maggie replied, "it was."

She stared at Galen. In the shadows, his face seemed to wear a mockingly amused mask, but he could not hide the bitterness in his voice. It echoed in her ears and tore at her heart, the anger that she had worked so hard to generate evaporating like mist. It was all she could do to keep from throwing her arms around him and telling him she wished with all her heart that she had spent the evening with him. Being near him made her tired body come alive, pulses racing, rejuvenated with the warmth that flowed from him in spite of his stony face.

"I wish I'd known where you lived," she said, trying to convey at least part of what she felt so that he would stop looking at her like that. "I'd have been here hours ago. I was bored to death."

"Really?' Galen raised his eyebrows skeptically. "Well, be that as it may, perhaps we'd better deal with your problem. Where's the car? I assume it's your parents'?"

"Down to the corner, then a couple of blocks that way," Maggie said, pointing. "But honestly, Galen, I can't walk back there. I'm getting blisters from these shoes and I think one of the heels came loose when I fell."

"No wonder," Galen said, looking down at them. "You'd better come inside while I go and change your tire. Can you walk that far?"

"Oh, sure," Maggie said quickly. She looked down as the dog who had frightened her so badly licked her hand. "This is quite a watchdog you have," she commented.

"Betsy's not usually so violent," Galen said, "but she's just had pups. She won't even let me near them yet."

"Bless her heart," Maggie said, patting the dog's large head. "I don't blame you, girl. You're just trying to be a good mama, aren't you? Is she a Labrador?"

"Part," Galen replied tersely, leading the way up the steps to a side door, which opened into his kitchen. He followed Maggie inside.

"Help yourself to some coffee," he said, jerking his thumb toward a large automatic coffeemaker on the counter. "If you'll give me the keys, I'll get to work." Noticing that Maggie was standing and staring at his paper-strewn table he added, "I was working on a brief."

"I . . . I'm sorry I interrupted you," Maggie said, trying to maintain her equilibrium while suddenly having one of the strangest sensations she'd ever experienced. She had glanced around the big, old-fashioned kitchen with its white-painted cabinets, its blue countertop and white enameled sink, the square oak table littered with Galen's work, the plain oak chairs, and had an almost perfect déjà vu, as if she had been awakened from a long, frightening dream and found herself safely in her own home. It made her dizzy, and she closed her eyes and clutched at the back of a chair for support.

"What's wrong, Maggie?" Galen asked, bending to peer into her face.

"N-nothing," she whispered. "Just a little dizzy."

"Sit down," he commanded, pulling out a chair and helping her into it. He poured a cup of coffee and set it in front of her. "That ought to help," he said. "You probably had a little too much to drink at Bruce's."

"I did not!" Maggie cried, tears springing to her eyes. "All I had was one glass of champagne, hours ago. I never drink anything strong."

Suddenly it was unbearable that Galen was still looking at her like that, his face, shadowed with a day's beard, still icy cold. She put her face down against her arms, her shoulders shaking with silent sobs.

"Good Lord," Galen said. He pulled Maggie's coat from her limp form, then sat beside her and put his arm around her shoulders. "I'm sorry," he said gently. "I didn't mean to sound so harsh. Are you ill?"

Maggie lifted her head and looked at him through her tears. He didn't seem cross with her now. She couldn't bear it when he was. "No," she whispered. Unless it was being ill to want so much to be in his arms that every inch of her body was trembling. She tried to hold very still as he put his hand on her forehead, but she could feel a shiver run through her at his touch.

"No temperature, but you're shaking and your forehead feels a little clammy," he said. "Maybe you'd better lie down for a while."

Galen's eyes were soft and warm now. "I'll be all right," Maggie said. As long as he looked at her like that, she would be. She picked up the coffee cup and gave him a wavering smile. "This coffee ought to fix me up."

"If you say so," Galen said. He studied Maggie's face, then sighed. "If you'll give me those keys now, I'll have a look at the tire."

"Isn't there someone we could call?" Maggie said, not wanting Galen to leave. "I don't even know if there's a good spare."

"I'll check it out first. If there isn't we'll have to call someone, but at this hour on a Saturday night, I'm not sure we'll get very fast results." Galen smiled wryly. "This isn't New York City."

Maggie reluctantly took the keys from her purse. "If it was, you'd wait until next week, and all they'd find would be the spot where the car used to be. Here." She put the keys into Galen's hand. "Please don't fuss with it if it looks like a terrible job," she said.

Galen's hand folded over the keys. "Are you afraid I'm not up to it?" he asked, some of the chill returning to his expression.

"No!" Tears sprang to Maggie's eyes again and she rubbed her hand across them impatiently. What was wrong with her? She sniffed and shook her head, words coming out of her tight throat in little spasms. "It's just that it's...the middle of the night, and it's a stupid, messy job, and...and..." she buried her face in her hands. "I'm so confused," she sobbed.

The keys hit the table with a clatter. Maggie felt strong arms close around her as Galen gathered her up and pulled her onto his lap. "Don't cry, baby," he murmured against her ear, smoothing her hair soothingly. "Damned if I know what's wrong, but we'll talk about it in the morning. You look exhausted. I think what you need first is a good night's sleep. I'm going to put you to bed in my guest room. Put your arms around my neck, now. Okay?"

For a moment, as Maggie saw Galen reach for his cane, she thought of telling him that she could walk, but immediately thought better of it. Her arms stole around his neck and she sighed contentedly, her head nestled against his shoulder. "I'm sorry to be so much trouble," she murmured, already feeling drowsy and warm.

"If this is trouble, I'd like to have more of it," Galen said dryly, carefully adjusting his balance and starting up the stairs. When they reached the top, he carried Maggie into a small bedroom, sparely furnished with a dark pine bed with a white spread, a dresser and rocking chair, bright red-checked curtains and a braided rug. He carefully lowered Maggie to sit on the side of the bed. "Will you be all right while I find you something to put on?" he asked, his hands holding her shoulders as he bent to look into her eyes.

Maggie smiled shyly and nodded. When Galen left the room, she looked around her. The ceiling was high, trimmed with shining dark woodwork. The walls were covered in a faintly patterned paper in shades of white and cream. There were two primitive prints of country scenes on the walls, a silver-framed picture of Galen's mother with one of her horses on the dresser. Again Maggie had an overwhelming sense of being somewhere she had been before, a place she belonged. Why should that be? She had never seen this house before, but if she had imagined a house for Galen, it would be just like this, solid and comfortable, not fancy or pretentious. She heard Galen's footsteps on the oak floor of the hallway and turned toward the door.

"Maybe this will do," he said, holding out a large red sweatshirt toward her as he crossed the room to her side. "I'm a little short on ladies' nightgowns."

"This is perfect," Maggie said, clutching the soft shirt to her and smiling at him. "Thank you."

Galen sat beside her and cradled her face in the palm of one large hand. He spoke slowly and carefully, as if he were talking to a child. "Does your mother expect you home tonight?" he asked.

"Yes, but I told her not to wait up," Maggie answered. Galen had the most beautiful eyes in the world. She could look at them forever.

"I'll call her first thing in the morning," Galen said. "Did you lock the car?"

"Yes," Maggie answered. He had the most beautiful mouth, too. She wanted to touch it with her fingertip and see if it was as soft and warm as it looked.

"I'll take care of that, too," Galen said. "Don't worry about it. There's a bathroom next door, with fresh towels and a new toothbrush for you if you want it. Is there anything else you need?"

"I don't think so," Maggie said. Except for you to kiss me, her mind continued.

"Good. Now, I want you to go to sleep and sleep as long as you like. If I should be gone when you wake up, it will only be for a few minutes while I look after your car. All right?"

"Yes," Maggie answered. She put her hand up and caught Galen's hand where it lay warm against her cheek. "Thank you," she said.

Galen smiled and shook his head, his eyes sparkling with bright shafts of inner sunlight. "I can't believe this is happening," he said. He bent his head and brushed Maggie's lips with a soft kiss. "I hope you sleep well. You look tired."

"I will," Maggie said. Impulsively she threw her arms around Galen's neck and pressed her cheek to his. Tears sprang to her eyes once more. *I'm in love with him,* she thought. *I'm absolutely crazy in love with him.*

She released him and a great shuddering sigh escaped her. "I am tired," she said shakily. "I haven't been sleeping very well lately." Because she was so stupid. She hadn't realized . . .

"Good night, Maggie," Galen said softly.

"Good night, Galen," she replied. She watched him leave the room, her heart so full of love she thought it would burst. Then she got ready for bed, snuggled under the warm woolly blanket and fell almost instantly into a deep, dreamless sleep.

IT WAS BRIGHT DAYLIGHT when Maggie opened her eyes. She blinked. Outside the window, she could see blue sky through the branches of a large tree. A large tree? There was no tree . . .

Everything came back to her in a flash. She smiled, turned over on her back and wriggled contentedly. She felt so good and warm and relaxed, as if she were floating on her own special cloud. How long had she slept? Poor Galen. He must have thought she'd lost her mind.

She hadn't. She'd only lost her heart. And she didn't miss it a bit. She closed her eyes, remembering how gently Galen had taken her into his arms, how comforting his strength had been when he carried her up the stairs and into this room. He'd seemed so worried about her. He must care about her, too, at least a little. As soon as he saw she wasn't feeling well, he wasn't angry anymore.

Maggie heard the sound of footsteps on the stairs and opened her eyes again. It was probably way past time she got up, she thought, listening to the footsteps coming closer. They paused outside her door. The doorknob turned silently, the door opened slowly, and Galen's head poked through the opening.

"Hi," Maggie said, smiling at him. "I just woke up."

Galen pushed the door open and came into the room. "How do you feel this morning?" he asked, coming to stand beside the bed.

"Much better," Maggie replied, her heart singing at the sight of him. He was clean-shaven now, dressed in jeans and a bright plaid flannel shirt. He looked quite serious, but his beautiful eyes were warm and bright. "Is it very late?" she asked.

"Almost noon," he replied, smiling. "Are you hungry?"

"Famished," she said. She was more hungry for a kiss than food, but she could see that Galen was not going to take advantage of her position to approach her that way, even though she thought she saw him making a deliberate effort to keep his eyes focused on hers.

"That's a good sign," Galen said. "I'll go downstairs and start cooking while you get dressed. Does bacon and eggs and fresh cinnamon rolls sound good?"

"Terrific," Maggie replied. "I'll just be a few minutes. I'll be glad to help." Then, as Galen started for the door, she glanced at the chair where she'd laid her clothes the night before. She couldn't put on that outfit! "Wait!" she called.

"What is it?" Galen asked, frowning as he turned back.

Maggie sat up and waved her hand toward her slinky black dress. "I can't put that on this morning. Have you got anything I could put on instead?"

Galen scratched his head. "Lord, Maggie, I don't know—"

"I know," she interrupted with a sudden inspiration. "I can leave this sweatshirt on. Do you have any sweatpants? The kind with a drawstring waist?"

"Yeah." Galen grinned. "That's going to be some outfit. Hold on a minute." He returned shortly with a pair of gray sweatpants and tossed them to her. "There you go. Don't stretch them out of shape."

"If I do, I'll buy you a new pair," Maggie promised, laughing.

She quickly showered and put on her lacy underthings, then added the huge shirt and baggy pants, which, she thought, thanks to their elastic ankles, looked like heavy-weight harem pants. She was in too much of a hurry to be back with Galen to bother with makeup, so, barefooted, she pattered down the stairs and through the hall past the living room and dining room to the kitchen.

"Ta da!" she said, holding her arms out and whirling around in her best model poses.

Galen stared at her, grinning, and shook his head. "I don't know how you do it, but you manage to make even that ridiculous outfit look chic. Are your feet cold?"

"No, I go barefoot all the time," Maggie replied. "What can I do to help?"

"Get the butter and orange juice out of the refrigerator," Galen said, removing several strips of bacon from a large iron frying pan. "The eggs will be ready in a jiffy."

Maggie found the requested items and set them on the table next to a plate of warm cinnamon rolls. Galen had already set their places with silverware in a plain Early American pattern, bright yellow place mats, white paper napkins and brown-rimmed coffee mugs.

"Shall I pour the coffee?" she asked, spotting the coffee maker on the counter.

"Yes, ma'am, please," Galen replied, carefully turning the eggs. "Do you take cream or sugar?"

"No, black," Maggie said. She carried the pot to the table and filled their cups, replaced it on the warmer, then sat down, leaning on her elbows and watching Galen contentedly. What a man. She would be perfectly happy to spend the rest of her life watching him make breakfast, or having him watch her. If only...

She sighed. If only all the other things that complicated her life would just go away.

"Here you go," Galen said, putting a plate of bacon and eggs in front of her. "I hope you like your eggs that way. It's the way I always do them, and I forgot to ask."

"Just the way I like them," she replied, smiling. "They look wonderful."

They ate for a while in silence until Galen broke the silence with a soft whistle. When Maggie looked up at him he grinned and gestured toward her clean plate. "I was going to ask if everything was all right, but either it was or you were too hungry to complain."

"It was marvelous," she replied, smiling. "In fact, I think I'll have some more coffee and another one of those rolls. Did you make them, too?"

"No, the bakery did," Galen replied, "but I have been known to try yeast breads. Didn't turn out too badly, if I do say so myself. I'll have some coffee, too."

"Amazing," Maggie said, bending close to him and refilling his cup. She caught a faint whiff of piney aftershave, and she inhaled deeply before she filled her own cup. When she had sat down again, she took another roll and started to butter it, feeling Galen's eyes watching her intently. "What?" she asked, raising her eyebrows.

"Just wondering how on earth you stay so thin," he answered.

"Not this way," she said. "I must have gained five pounds since I got home, but I don't care. I'm tired of dieting all the time. I like good food."

"Tired of modeling?" Galen asked.

There was a serious note in his voice. Was he hoping she was? Maggie wondered. She glanced at him, then studied her roll before she answered, thinking aloud and choosing her words carefully. "I'm getting that way. The thrill is gone. At first it was all new and exciting, but it's pretty routine now. And, I'm twenty-seven. Models aren't necessarily over the hill at thirty anymore, but it gets tougher to compete, and I don't want to play that game. There's got to be something more rewarding I can do with the rest of my life."

"Like getting married and raising a family?" Galen asked.

A current of electricity sent Maggie's pulse racing. This was almost like a fencing match, she thought. Neither of them was saying exactly what they meant. "I'd like that to be part of my future," she answered evenly, looking at Galen.

Galen dropped his eyes and took a swallow of his coffee. "I'm glad to hear that," he said dryly. "I was afraid you were planning to spend the rest of your life modeling and sparkling and glittering on Roger Balfour's arm until someday I saw this gray-haired woman I used to know grinning at me from the cover of *Modern Maturity*. So Roger wants to have a family?" He cocked an eyebrow at Maggie.

She bit her lip and looked down. Why did Galen have to bring up Roger and spoil her lovely morning? As to his question, that was something that she and Roger had never discussed, but she knew with a sudden certainty that he did not, nor would she want to have his children if he did. Loving Galen made that impossible. It made marrying Roger impossible. She was going to have to tell him that soon.

"I'm sorry if that question was too personal," Galen said, interrupting her thoughts. "I didn't mean to pry."

"That wasn't it," Maggie said quickly. She shrugged and made a face. "We've never discussed it at all. I was just thinking..." She bit her lip again. Should she tell Galen she'd decided not to marry Roger? She doubted he'd tell anyone, but still she owed it to Roger to tell him first. "I was thinking that I...have some big decisions to make," she finished, popping the last bite of roll into her mouth.

"Mmm," Galen murmured. "Is that what had you so upset last night? You said you were confused."

"I guess maybe that was part of it," Maggie confessed. She hadn't thought about it then, but confusion had been building inside her ever since she'd arrived home. She sighed. "I'm worried about Bruce, too. He's not the brother I used to know. And—" she smiled wryly "—I really did have a rotten time at his party. I wanted to have a good time, but it just didn't happen."

"I've been to parties like that," Galen said with a smile.

The sound of honking came from the driveway.

"That will be your car coming back," Galen said. "There wasn't any spare, and the tires were so bad that I had them tow it in and put on a new set. I should have noticed the tires before when I was visiting your parents."

"I wish I'd paid more attention, too," Maggie said. She gave Galen an impish smile. "I can't say I'm really sorry I had that flat last night, though."

"Neither am I," he replied soberly, "but if you'd had it out in the country you'd have been very sorry. You could have had a bad accident."

"I know," she said. And now the car was here and she could go back to Spring Mountain, something she did not want to do at all at the moment. "I guess I'll have to go pretty soon, but can I help clean up the dishes first?" she asked hopefully.

"I'd appreciate it," Galen said.

Galen filled half of the double sink with sudsy water and handed Maggie a dish towel. They worked silently, side by side, Maggie so aware of Galen's nearness that she was afraid her hands would tremble and she would drop a plate. When the last dish was dried, she hung up the towel and turned toward Galen.

"Well, I guess that does it," she said.

"I guess it does," he replied. His eyes scanned her face, a small worried frown making a crease between his dark brows.

"Is something wrong?" Maggie asked. Could it be that Galen didn't want her to leave?

"I hope not," Galen said. He took a deep breath. "I was wondering if I dared ask you one more time if you'd drive out to the hills with me. It's a beautiful day, and..."

Maggie suddenly realized that she'd been holding her breath, for she involuntarily took in a deep breath and her heart started racing. "I'd love to," she said. Then she looked down. "Good Lord, I'd scare people looking like this."

"There's a discount store at the shopping center," Galen suggested. "Nothing fancy, but you might be able to find something to wear. I need to stop and pick up a few groceries to take along, and some toys for the kids."

"I'll get my shoes," Maggie said quickly. "I just hope they'll let me in the store to get what I need."

A short time later, Maggie had acquired a pair of jeans, a blue sweater and a lightweight jacket, as well as tennis shoes and socks. People had stared at her, but she had ignored them, thankful that it wasn't New York where someone might have called the newspapers to have a photographer catch her looking like a scarecrow. Galen bought two large bags of groceries, and small toys for children of several different ages.

"Is that all for one particular family?" Maggie asked him as they started off again.

Galen nodded grimly. "Their name is Bryant. John's been unemployed for a couple of years. He used to drive trucks for a mine that closed down. The mother, Susan is a nice little person, but she's pretty depressed now. They can barely keep food on the table and clothes on the four little kids, not to mention trying to keep a car running so they can take two of them to the hospital several times a month. The baby has a heart defect, and the oldest—" Galen paused and grimaced "—is an adorable little girl who has leukemia. She was in remission until about a month ago, but now she's back on heavy chemotherapy and it doesn't look very hopeful."

"How tragic," Maggie said. "It doesn't seem right that with all of the wealth in this country, we can't take better care of people than that." She glanced over at Galen, who had made an unpleasant snorting sound.

"There are some people," he said harshly, "who think it's not right that the Bryants and people like them should have four children to burden the rest of us with. But they were doing just fine, or thought they were, until John lost his job. Then within a year the baby was born damaged, and little Carrie's leukemia was discovered. The toxicologists and the courts felt that both problems could have been caused by the horrendous level of toxic waste that seeped into their well. Unfortunately there's no way of proving it with one hundred percent certainty, so meanwhile they wait and wait for their share of the judgment against Balfour."

Maggie looked out the window. From the way Galen had said "some people" she could tell he was including Roger Balfour in that group. She wished she could believe Roger didn't feel that way, but she couldn't, not anymore, and the thought saddened her. She shouldn't have had to wonder about it—she should have known. It had been so easy to forget that there were problems that needed solving, so much easier to respond with money than to really think about what she might do. No wonder Galen had doubted her sincerity.

The road turned and turned again, crossing a rushing stream on a rickety bridge. Then, at a crossroads with a combination general store and gasoline station, they took a gravel road that led them deep into a wooded hollow. The last part of the drive was on a lane barely scratched out of the hillside. It came to an end at a cabin where a scrawny hound came bounding out to meet them, and several chickens went squawking off toward a ramshackle shed where a goat was tethered. At the sound of Galen's car, the door of the cabin flew open, a small head peeped out, and two little boys came running toward them.

"You take the toys," Galen said to Maggie. "I think you can tell who gets which ones."

He got out and crouched down to give the two boys a warm embrace as they shouted, "Hi, Galen!" Their wide grins told Maggie that he was a familiar and much-loved friend. A moment later, a thin man and woman followed, the woman carrying a baby in her arms. Behind them came another child.

At the sight of the little girl, Maggie's heart ached. She was a beautiful child, her eyes wide and bright as the lovely smile she gave them, but her skin was pale, almost translucent, and her head was completely bald, a result, Maggie knew, of the chemotherapy.

"I've brought a new friend to meet you," Galen said to the children. "This is Maggie Preston. Maggie, meet Carrie and Johnny and Jeff. The baby is Sara. And the parents are John and Susan Bryant."

"Hello, everyone," Maggie said, smiling at the family, who more or less in unison said something like, "Pleased to meet you."

After that, Galen and John carried the groceries into the cabin, and Maggie followed, admiring the baby and bringing along the bag of toys. She distributed the two metal trucks to the boys, a stuffed toy rabbit to the baby and a little set of doll dishes to Carrie. The boys said a grave, "Thank you," but Carrie squealed enthusiastically.

"He remembered! I told Galen my doll didn't have any dishes," she explained to Maggie. "Now I can have real parties for her. Would you like to see my doll?"

"I'd love to," Maggie said, and Carrie hurried off. Maggie saw her mother watching her, the saddest look she had ever seen on her face, and felt tears prick her eyes. How could she bear it? Maggie wondered. She blinked the tears back and managed a bright smile when Carrie returned with an obviously much-loved doll with long curly blond hair.

"Galen brought her for my birthday," Carrie said, holding her out for Maggie to admire. "Mama's made her a nightie and a coat, too."

"She's lovely," Maggie said, taking the doll and cradling her in her hands. "I think she's about the prettiest doll I ever saw. What's her name?"

"Gale," Carrie said shyly. "I named her for Galen, 'cause he's so nice."

"That he is," Maggie agreed. He was a lot more than nice. He was probably the kindest, most compassionate man she'd ever known. How many more families, she wondered, did he help this way?

They stayed for almost an hour talking to the family. The boys climbed all over Galen, treating him like an adored uncle. Maggie wound up with the baby on her lap and Carrie standing beside her, touching Maggie's generous mane of hair enviously and wishing aloud that if her hair ever grew back again it would look like that. When they left, the whole family came outside again to see them off.

"Are you going to come again?" Carrie asked Maggie.

"Yes, I'll come again," Maggie promised. "What would you like next time? Anything special?"

"No." Carrie smiled wistfully. "Just to be here."

This time, Maggie could not stop the tears that sprang to her eyes. What in God's name could you say to that? She bent and took the little girl in her arms and held her close.

She got into the car, smiling and waving while the tears streamed silently down her cheeks. When they were well out of sight of the house, Galen stopped the car.

"Are you all right?" he asked, putting his hand over Maggie's.

Maggie shook her head. "No," she said hoarsely, "and I don't want to be. I don't ever want to forget again. How many more are there like Carrie?" She raised her head to look at Galen and was surprised to see him smiling radiantly at her. He caught her head with his hand and leaned over to kiss her lips so sweetly that Maggie could only stare at him, her heart full of love.

"That's the Maggie Preston I used to know," he said. He drew back and started the car moving again. "To answer your question a little vaguely, there are many more, not to mention the trees and birds and fish and other wildlife that have suffered, not only from waterborne but airborne pollution. And this is only one small area, in one state. It's getting better, but so slowly, and whenever the government lets up, nothing gets done." Then he looked at Maggie and gave her another brilliant smile. "How would you like to see a really pretty little waterfall?"

"I'd like to," Maggie replied. "Is it near here?"

"Not far," Galen said. "I discovered it the first time I came to see the Bryants and got a little lost."

They went to a crossroad, then took a turn just before a rickety bridge on a road that was barely more than two tire tracks between the trees. It climbed almost straight up a hill and came to a dead end, with nothing but trees all around them.

"Here we are. It's a short hike up the hill," Galen said.

"I'd say you were more than a little lost," Maggie commented as she got out of the car.

Galen laughed. "Just come with me," he said, taking her hand and holding it tightly in his.

The path he followed was almost too narrow for the two of them, but Maggie ducked under the lowest branches and managed to stay at Galen's side.

"Are you sure you know where you're going?" she asked, when they had to stop to untangle a branch from her hair.

"Absolutely," Galen said. "I can hear rushing water now. Can't you?"

Maggie listened intently. "I think so," she said. It was difficult to hear anything over the anticipatory pounding of her heart. Galen was taking her somewhere special, and maybe at the end of this trail she might find something even more exciting than a waterfall.

A short distance more and they came to a rocky outcropping hidden from view by the underbrush until they were almost upon it. The gray, moss- and lichen-covered rocks formed a small U no more than ten feet across that caught a little stream in a tiny pool and then let it tumble to another pool some twenty feet below them. The pungent smell of the forest responding to the warmth of spring hung softly in the still air. Shafts of sunlight through the trees were catching the droplets of water, creating brilliant little rainbows in the mist. A cardinal flashed scarlet across the tiny canyon. The raucous caw of a crow sounded briefly higher up the mountain, then all was still again except for the sound of the falling water.

"It's beautiful," Maggie said softly.

"It's even prettier when the spring flowers come along," Galen said. "First the bloodroot, then the hepatica and trillium, later the rhododendrons. We'll have to come back then."

Galen edged out to the brink and sat, helping Maggie down beside him. He put his arm around her and pulled her against his shoulder. "I always come here after I've seen the Bryants," he said. "It helps me get my perspective back, so I realize I can't solve all the world's problems and it will go on without me whether I do or not."

He looked at Maggie. "It's very special to have you here with me," he said. "I don't know if you realize it or not, but after my accident, you helped me get my perspective back. I don't think I'd have made it without you."

"Oh, Galen," Maggie whispered, laying her hand along his cheek, tears stinging her eyes. "That's the most wonderful thing anyone ever told me."

She held her breath, watching the flickering lights deep in the cool gray depths of Galen's eyes. He let his eyes travel down to her lips. Her hand crept around behind his neck, gently pulling him toward her. Their lips met, and a soaring happiness filled Maggie's heart. As Galen deepened the kiss, Maggie burrowed into the strong enclosure of his arms, answering the passionate intensity of his exploration with her own. She needed him, she wanted him, more than she had thought it possible to want a man. She sighed dreamily as together they lay back against the woodsy carpet, Maggie cradled in the curve of Galen's shoulder. Above, a hawk circled effortlessly in the blue sky. She looked at Galen and smiled.

"Still heavenly, isn't it?" he murmured, his lips nibbling softly at hers.

"Uh-huh," she replied, gazing star-struck into the velvet softness of his eyes. She wanted so much to press against him, to let him know even more clearly how much she wanted him, but was afraid to move and break the spell. Galen would lead and she must follow. He had known where he wanted to take her all along.

His finger traced the outline of her jaw, then he made a fist and touched it lightly under her chin. "I think we'd better be going back," he said, smiling at her as he drew back. "It's getting late."

Reluctantly Maggie got to her feet and followed Galen to his car. If only she really understood what he was doing, she thought. He seemed to have his own agenda, of which he was perfectly sure. Where did she fit into his plans?

CHAPTER SIX

THE STREETLIGHTS were coming on when Maggie and Galen arrived at his house.

"I'd better call Mom and tell her I'll be late for dinner," Maggie said. "It's been a wonderful day. I don't know how to thank you for...for everything." She smiled wryly. "I guess maybe the best thing I could do is to apologize for making it so hard for you to show me how stupid I was."

"I never thought you were stupid, Maggie," Galen said. "A little confused and misguided, maybe, but not stupid." He unlocked the side door to his house and let Maggie precede him into the kitchen. "You know," he said thoughtfully, as Maggie headed for the telephone, "we could send out for some Chinese food. I don't know about you, but I'm starving. It's been a long time since we ate, and if you drive home, you won't get to eat for a couple of hours yet."

"That sounds great!" Maggie said quickly, a warm glow filling her at the knowledge that Galen apparently didn't want her to leave any more than she wanted to go.

"Let me at the phone," Galen said, moving past her. "I have a regular place I call. Best Chinese east of Shanghai." He had lifted his hand to pick up the telephone when it rang. Frowning, he picked up the receiver.

"Hello?" There was a long pause on Galen's end, during which Maggie watched his frown grow darker, his mouth draw into a tight line. He picked up a notepad, scribbled something on it, then stuffed it into his pocket. "Got it," he said cryptically, then hung up the phone. He took a deep breath, obviously trying to compose himself, then shook his head.

"Something's come up," he said, and Maggie could tell from the way his eyes flashed restlessly around the room that it was something important. His mind was already working on whatever it was, his look distracted. He saw her watching him and glanced quickly at his watch. "I'm going to have to leave in about fifteen minutes. I'm sorry. Shall we have a cup of coffee before you go?"

"All right," Maggie agreed. She watched as Galen poured a cup of leftover coffee then set it to warm in the microwave. "Does this sort of thing happen often?" she asked. "Being called out late in the day like Perry Mason on a hot lead?"

Galen gave a short laugh. "No, at least not often enough to make a TV series out of it." He set a cup in front of Maggie, then put another in to warm.

He seemed very tense. "It isn't dangerous, is it?" she asked.

"Not likely," Galen replied. He stood silently waiting for the chime of the microwave's clock, then took his coffee and sat next to Maggie. "I'm really sorry we couldn't have dinner together," he said, reaching over to squeeze her hand, "but we'll do it next time you come home. I'm afraid I'm tied up all week."

"Even at night?" Maggie asked wistfully. "Don't you ever rest?"

Galen smiled. "I don't work all night, but when I do get through I'm not very good company. I'd rather not subject you to my worst side. I'll be working on something I can't discuss with anyone for a while, or it might be different."

"Something to do with the case against Balfour?" Maggie hazarded. That would certainly explain why he wouldn't want to discuss it with her.

"Can't say," Galen replied with a shrug. "When do you think you'll be home again?"

"I'm not sure." Maggie bit her lip and looked down. Lord, but it was frustrating not being able to tell Galen that she had decided not to marry Roger. If he knew that, his whole attitude might be different. How could she give him a clue?

"I...I have a pretty busy schedule for the next month," she said slowly, "but after that...I may decide to come home for good." She looked up at Galen, hoping to see his face light up with a smile. Instead, he looked worried.

"You'd better think about that very carefully," he said seriously. "After all, you have a lot invested in your career, and you'd take a tremendous cut in pay if you came back to West Virginia, whatever you decided to do instead of modeling. Not to mention the fact that the bright lights and glamour would be virtually nonexistent."

Stung, Maggie had to look away to prevent Galen from seeing the hurt she felt. Did he really think all she wanted to do was change careers? Or did he want her to know that she'd better not count on anything else?

"Don't worry," she said tightly, "I won't make any hasty decisions." She gave him a defiant glance. "And if I do come back, I'll have a nest egg that would keep most people for a lifetime, so you needn't worry about my starving."

"I'm glad to hear you've managed your money well," Galen said. He looked at his watch and got quickly to his feet. "I've got to be going. Drive carefully. I'll keep in touch with your parents. They can tell me when you'll be coming back."

"I do have a telephone, you know," Maggie said, pausing at the doorway. "And I could call you, too."

Galen shook his head firmly. "No, don't do that. There's a chance that my phone might be bugged. It isn't now, but it could happen, and it wouldn't do for us to be communicating."

"I don't understand," Maggie said, following him down the stairs to the driveway. "Who would do that? It's illegal, isn't it?"

"Yes, but that doesn't stop some people," Galen said. He turned and took Maggie's shoulders in his hands. "Don't mention it, for God's sake. Don't tell anyone I told you that. All right?" When Maggie nodded, he smiled suddenly. "I'm terribly sorry such a great day had to end this way. Don't look so worried. This isn't some big murder mystery—it's fairly routine. I'm just very careful." He bent his head and gave her a quick kiss. "Take care, Maggie," he said softly, then turned and hurried to his car.

Mystified, Maggie watched him back his car out and pull away with a screech of the tires. She shook her head, went into the house to collect her things, got into her parents' car and began the long drive back to Spring Mountain, suddenly feeling very tired and let down. Galen hadn't seemed very enthusiastic about the idea of her coming home to stay. She'd have sworn that he would have been after all the things he'd said about her getting her heart and mind moving in the same direction. Was it only because he wasn't sure how strong her commitment to Roger Balfour was? Did he think she might change her mind when she got back to New York and want to protect himself against possible disappointment?

"I hope that's it," Maggie muttered. She'd like it a lot better if he'd simply declare himself her suitor and join the battle, like a knight of old ready to joust for his lady fair. As it was, he didn't even want to talk to her on the telephone. His excuse about the bugged phone didn't make much sense. What person criminal enough to bug a phone would care if he talked to her? Unless—Maggie shuddered at the thought—Roger or some of his associates dealt in that kind of thing. Could it be that she didn't really know Roger at all? Could Galen be in real danger? If anything happened to Galen and she found out that Roger was involved . . .

The thought of holding her old hunting rifle with the cross hairs centered on Roger flitted through her mind. She shook her head and passed a trembling hand across her forehead. That was ridiculous. Too much melodrama on TV had gotten to her.

When Maggie arrived in Spring Mountain, she found her mother anxiously waiting by the door. "Thank goodness!" she said. "Where have you been? I tried to call Galen's house this afternoon and there wasn't any answer, and I tried again about an hour ago. I even called Bruce, just to see if you'd gone back there."

A sick knot formed in Maggie's stomach. "You didn't tell Bruce I'd stayed at Galen's last night, did you?" she demanded.

"Well, I had to," her mother said defensively. "I had to explain why I wondered where you were."

Maggie took a deep breath and counted to ten. "Mother," she said as calmly as she could, "I would appreciate it if you'd stop worrying about me as if I were a child. Your car is back safe and sound, with a new set of tires, thanks to Galen. I can imagine what Bruce had to say."

"I wouldn't care to repeat it," her mother said with a grimace. "I just don't know what's gotten into that boy. I don't like the way he's acting lately at all."

"Neither do I," Maggie said. "I'm going to try and have a talk with him one day this week, if he'll be calm and rational."

"I doubt if he will be," Mrs. Preston said. "He said he was going to track you down and give you a piece of his mind, but you seem to have missed him. What did you and Galen do? Go out for dinner?"

"No. In fact I haven't had any dinner," Maggie replied. "Do you have any leftovers, or shall I make myself a sandwich?"

"There's cold fried chicken and potato salad in the refrigerator," her mother answered. "What did you and Galen do all day?"

"Talked a lot," Maggie replied as she took the food out and found herself a plate.

"That's not much of an answer," her mother said, sitting down opposite Maggie at the table and eyeing her suspiciously.

"Mother! I am not going to discuss it with you, period," Maggie said as patiently as she could manage. "How's Dad?"

"As well as could be expected," her mother said, giving Maggie a disapproving frown. "He's been just as worried as I have, but he's gone to sleep in front of the TV again. Nervous exhaustion, I expect."

"No doubt," Maggie said, trying to hide a smile. Her mother was trying to make her feel guilty, as if she were still a teenager. Fortunately it didn't work anymore, and she was not going to tell her a thing about her day with Galen. The less she knew, the less she could tell Bruce and aggravate him even more. "This is awfully good chicken," she said, polishing off her second piece. "Great potato salad, too."

"Humph. You don't need to think you can butter me up that way," Mrs. Preston said, but Maggie could see she was weakening.

"Okay, I won't," Maggie agreed. "Just be sure to make it again before I leave, so I can have it when it's hot."

"If I know when you'll be here," her mother said, giving Maggie a sideways glance.

At that, Maggie laughed outright. "You'll know," she said. "I think I'll go and wake Dad up now and relieve his anxiety."

Maggie and her father had just gotten well into a game of gin rummy when the telephone rang and Mrs. Preston called to Maggie from the kitchen. "Maggie! Bruce wants to talk to you."

"Oh, great!" Maggie frowned. "Tell him I'll call him some day soon. I'm busy." She had no desire to listen to one of Bruce's tirades.

"He says he wants to talk to you right now," her mother said seconds later.

"Hang up on him," Maggie suggested.

"I can't do that."

With a sigh, Maggie got up and went to the telephone. "Hello, Bruce," she said. "What's up?"

"What's up?" Bruce's voice sounded like raw fury. "What in hell were you thinking of, Maggie, spending the night and day with Galen Kendrick? Haven't you any idea of the kind of situation you're apt to find yourself in if Roger Balfour finds out?''

Maggie gritted her teeth and tried to control her temper. ''Bruce, I did not sleep with Galen, if that's what you think, and as for any quote situation unquote, I have no idea what you're talking about. Besides, I can't think of any reason for Roger to find out—unless you tell him. Do you plan to do that?''

''Of course not!'' Bruce snapped. ''But you never know who might have seen you when you were out and about with him today. Where did you go, anyway?''

''That's none of your business,'' Maggie said coldly. ''Furthermore, I don't like this kind of inquisition from you, and I won't put up with it. I think it's time we had a little talk. Let's meet for lunch one day this week.''

''All right, but I think you're the one who needs talking to,'' Bruce said. ''There's a quiet place called the Red Duck near the plant. That should be a good spot. I'll make reservations. How about Tuesday?''

''That's all right with me.''

''Okay, see you then. In the meantime, stay away from Galen!''

''Bruce?'' Maggie said softly.

''What?''

''Shut up!'' she shouted, and banged down the receiver.

''Be careful,'' her mother said, frowning, ''you'll break the telephone.''

''I'd like to break Bruce's neck,'' Maggie replied. ''If he doesn't straighten out, I may do exactly that.''

By the time Maggie reached the restaurant in Charleston on Tuesday, she had calmed down somewhat, but she still felt angry every time she thought of

Bruce's nerve in telling her how to run her life. The weather had warmed, and she was wearing a trim beige suit with a black turtleneck sweater beneath it and no jewelry. Men stared at her, as they always did, while she stood in the foyer waiting for Bruce to arrive. She ignored them, but felt more irritated by it than usual. Men! She was fed up with Bruce, disgusted with Roger and all he seemed to stand for, and worried about Galen. Was he, perhaps, in over his head in trying to deal with Roger Balfour and his powerful interests?

"Oh, there you are," she said, frowning at Bruce when he arrived. "You're late."

"Only a couple of minutes," Bruce said, glancing at his watch. "You look like you're in a lousy mood."

"I am," Maggie said. "Watch out." She was pleased to see that Bruce looked at her a little anxiously. Maybe little sister hadn't lost her ability to intimidate him, after all. Even though Bruce was three years older than she, she had always been more quick-witted and had frequently succeeded in getting him into trouble he didn't really deserve.

The hostess led them to a table in a far corner of the restaurant. "Would you like anything from the bar?" she asked.

"No, thank you," Maggie replied.

"A Scotch on the rocks," Bruce answered without looking at Maggie.

"Dutch courage, or do you always drink at lunchtime?" Maggie asked coolly.

"Now, look Maggie," Bruce said, "if you're spoiling for a fight—"

"Not particularly," Maggie interrupted, "but may I hasten to remind you that if I am, you started it. However, I did not come here to discuss my relationship with

Galen or Roger or anyone else. It is none of your business."

"Like hell it isn't," Bruce said, taking a large swallow of his drink as soon as it was set in front of him. "I don't like to see my only sister making a fool of herself."

Maggie eyed him narrowly. "Why is it I doubt your concern is for my reputation and well-being? Why is it I wonder how you can afford that fancy apartment and car, and am beginning to suspect that your concern has more to do with that than anything else?"

That, she thought grimly, really hit the mark. Bruce couldn't even look her in the eye. When he said nothing she went on. "Bruce, if you've got a problem, I wish you'd tell me about it. I'm actually quite wealthy. I've taken Roger's advice on some investments, but I've gotten independent verification, too, and I've never taken a penny from Roger. What I have is all mine."

Bruce's mouth tightened into a grim line. "The problem goes deeper than that, Maggie," he said, "but I can't talk about it. All I can say is that I want you to go ahead and let Roger buy you that ring, and not rock the boat."

"What if I decide not to?" Maggie asked, studying Bruce's face carefully. At her words, a look of sheer fear came into his eyes and he paled visibly.

"You're not thinking of changing your mind?" he asked hoarsely.

"Bruce, I've never told him I would," Maggie replied. "As to what I may do in the future, that's my business alone. I suggest you'd better get your affairs arranged so that your future isn't dependent on mine. You have no right to ask me to commit myself for the rest of my life in order to keep your life running smoothly.''

Bruce's mouth twisted wryly and he shook his head. "You don't understand, Maggie," he said. "But I guess you're right."

The waitress brought their lunch, but for the first time in days Maggie had no appetite. The frightened look on Bruce's face troubled her deeply. What kind of hold did Roger have over him, and why did so much depend on her marrying Roger? She would, she thought, find out before very long. The next time she saw Roger, she was going to tell him she was not going to marry him.

Maggie managed to eat part of her shrimp salad, but Bruce scarcely touched his, downing another Scotch instead. "Bruce," she said, reaching over and taking hold of his hand, "I'm really worried about you. Don't you realize that all the beautiful things you have don't really mean anything unless you're happy? Wouldn't it be better just to get whatever it is off your chest, take your lumps if need be, even start all over from scratch if you have to?"

Bruce looked down at Maggie's slender hand on top of his, then abruptly pulled his hand away. "No," he said, "it wouldn't be."

"But why?" Maggie persisted.

"I expect you'll find out soon enough," Bruce replied. He raised watery eyes to Maggie's and shook his head. "Please, whatever happens, try not to hate me."

"I could never hate you," Maggie said, appalled at the tortured look on Bruce's face. Whatever was wrong, it was tearing her brother apart and he refused to let her help him. "Bruce," she said gently, finally voicing the idea that had been gnawing at her, "what kind of hold does Roger have over you? What have you done?"

Bruce stared at her, his face suddenly so different it was as if he had shed a layer of skin. "Don't even think that, Maggie," he said, leaning toward her and fixing her with an intent, narrow-eyed look, "and for God's sake don't say any such thing to Roger. Okay?"

Maggie nodded, at the same time trying to figure out why Bruce should have turned from anxious to angrily commanding in a split second. "Okay, but I wish you'd tell me—"

"Soon," Bruce said. He glanced at his watch and stood up. "I've got to get back to work. It's been good talking to you, Maggie. Don't look so worried. I'll be all right."

Maggie tried to smile brightly. "I'm sure you will," she said, but her voice lacked conviction.

She went to her car, feeling more confused and depressed than she could ever remember being. What could be going on between Bruce and Roger that could make Bruce imagine she might come to hate him? It must be something illegal, but what? If only she had someone to talk to who might help her find a clue. If only she and Galen were the ones talking of marriage, she would have his broad shoulders to lean on.

The thought of Galen brought his image to Maggie's mind. How she'd like to at least see him and know that there was someone in the world she felt good about. She could stop by his office. He might be able to spare her a few minutes. Maggie glanced around, trying to get oriented. She knew the address of his law office. If she turned right at the next traffic light, she should be almost there.

A few minutes later, she had found the building with the sign Galen Kendrick, Attorney-at-Law by the door. She parked in front of it, but it took her several minutes to gather her courage to go in. He had said he'd be very busy, and all that she really wanted was to stare at him, like an addict in need of a fix. Still, she would like to see that he'd returned from whatever mysterious meeting he'd had on Sunday night without any problem. She could use that as an excuse. Finally she pushed open the car door and got out, walking slowly up to the heavy door of the old ornate brick building with its overhanging cornices and high narrow windows capped by decorative arches. It was, she thought, the right kind of place for Galen's office. A slick modern facility wouldn't suit him at all.

She opened the door and went inside. A severe-looking woman with gray hair pulled back in an old-fashioned bun looked up from her computer and raised her eyebrows.

"May I help you?" she asked.

"I...I'd like to see Mr. Kendrick, if he's in," Maggie said, the woman's cool look suddenly making her feel like a child in school who has been caught throwing spitballs behind the teacher's back.

"Mr. Kendrick is with a client," the woman said, "and he has a full schedule this afternoon. Perhaps you'd like to make an appointment?"

"Could I possibly wait and see him for just a minute between appointments?" Maggie asked, beginning to feel foolish but determined now that she'd gotten this far not to give up. "It's very important."

The woman's mouth tightened. "If you give me your name I'll ask," she said.

"Maggie Preston," Maggie replied.

"Oh." The woman looked surprised. "You're one of the Preston family from Spring Mountain?" When Maggie nodded, the woman's expression softened a little. "Do take a seat," she said, gesturing toward an armchair on the other side of the reception room. "He'll be out in a few minutes."

Maggie sat, musing wryly that it was rather nice to be identified as "one of the Preston family" instead of as "the famous model." It made her part of something, instead of standing alone and untouchable on some sort of pedestal.

Fifteen minutes passed, and Maggie was having second and third thoughts about her visit, when down a hallway to her left she heard a door open and the sound of Galen's voice. A moment later he appeared in the reception room, his arm around the shoulders of an anxious-looking young man.

"I'll be in touch as soon as the judge sets the court date," he said.

"Thanks. Thanks a lot for taking my case," the young man said, giving Galen a little smile. The two men shook hands, and the young man went out the door. Then Galen turned toward the reception room.

"Maggie! My God, what are you doing here?" he said, his dark eyebrows arched in surprise.

"Do you always have to say that when you see me?" Maggie asked, getting up and moving toward him. At that, Galen laughed heartily.

"Sorry," he said, "but you always turn up when I least expect you. Come on back to my office. I've got a few minutes before I have to go to the courthouse."

He put his arm casually around Maggie's shoulders and led her down the hallway and into his office. "Have a seat," he said, gesturing toward a leather upholstered chair on one side of a large cluttered desk. "What brings you here today? Need a good lawyer?"

Maggie shook her head, then gave a short laugh. "Maybe I do and I just don't know it. No, I was in the neighborhood and I wanted to see you so I could be sure you didn't run into any trouble Sunday night. I was worried."

"Thanks." Galen smiled warmly. "I'm not used to being worried about. I think I like it." Then he cocked his head and studied Maggie curiously. "You still look worried. Anything to do with the reason you're in Charleston today?"

Maggie looked down and fiddled with the strap of her purse. Galen could read her like a book. Should she tell him anything about her worries? Seeing him, feeling his arm around her, made her long even more for his help. She felt a childish desire to curl up on his lap and bury her face against his shoulder and have him pat her back and call her "baby" again. But it was her problem, and he was a very busy man. She took a deep breath.

"Yes," she said softly, "but it's nothing you can help with. I'm still worried about Bruce."

Galen nodded. "Go on. Tell me, anyway."

"Well..." Maggie looked at him, a rush of adoration filling her at the gentle kindness in his face. Afraid that he would be able to read that, too, she lowered her eyes again. "I'm afraid Bruce is in some kind of terrible trouble." She went on to tell Galen briefly about their conversation. "What could he possibly have done to make him think I could hate him?" she asked, her mind still trying to answer the question. "Could he have embezzled the money for all the things he has? Could Roger have found out and told him he'd not prosecute since he's my brother? That could explain why Bruce is so afraid of what will happen if I don't marry Roger."

Galen gave Maggie a brief intense look, then leaned on his elbows and laced his fingers together, studying his hands as he spoke. "Maggie," he said slowly, "I wish I could tell you that I don't think Bruce has a problem, but I can't. However, I wouldn't jump to any hasty conclusions. Just be prepared for any kind of revelation. Whether you marry Roger Balfour or not, it's bound to come out eventually."

"Oh, Lord," Maggie said, twisting her hands together. "it's hard for me to believe that Bruce would stoop to such a thing as embezzling. If he has, I blame myself for maybe leading him to think that money was terribly important."

"Don't do that," Galen said, looking at Maggie very seriously. "Bruce is a grown man, quite capable of making his own decisions. I think he'll come out of this all right."

"Do you know something I don't?" Maggie asked sharply.

Galen shook his head. "No. But I know Bruce pretty well."

"I thought I did," Maggie said with a sigh. "He ought to know that whatever he's done, I won't hate him."

"I don't think he really believes you will," Galen said comfortingly. "He's just feeling anxious about... something."

Maggie nodded. "I guess you're right. Well, if you hear anything at all, please let me know. I'd like to be able to break it to my parents gently. It would be terrible to have them learn it from something splashed all over the news."

"I'll keep my ear to the ground," Galen said. He glanced at his watch. "I've got to go," he said, getting up from his chair and reaching for his jacket. "I hope I haven't made things worse for you instead of better."

"You haven't," Maggie said, watching with an aching heart as he slipped his broad shoulders into a tan tweed jacket. She wanted so desperately to touch him and feel his arms around her again. He bent and picked up his briefcase.

"I guess I'm ready," he said, peering at the piles of papers on his desk. "I don't think I've forgotten anything." He looked at Maggie and smiled. "I'm sometimes worse than an absentminded professor."

"I believe it," Maggie said, smiling at him. He looked perfectly wonderful, except that he had loosened his tie while he talked to her and had forgotten to tighten it again. She moved quickly in front of him. "You did forget one little thing," she said, taking his tie in her hands and fixing it. "There. Now you look very distinguished."

"Thank you," Galen said, smiling at her. "My secretary usually has to remind me to do that. She'll know that I had help."

"Is she the jealous type?" Maggie asked, amused at the thought of the dour woman being interested in Galen.

Galen laughed. "She knows me too well for that. In fact, she tells me that a grouchy old workaholic like me should do all the ladies a favor and stay single, and I expect she's right."

Maggie's heart sank. All she needed to complete this dreadful day was for Galen to say something like that. She followed him out the door, biting her lip to fight back the tears that threatened.

When they reached her car, Galen stopped. "Take care, Maggie. I'll see you before too long," he said.

"Yeah. I'll see you later," Maggie muttered without looking up. She started to walk away, but felt a strong hand grab her arm to stop her.

"Maggie, look at me," Galen commanded.

Slowly Maggie raised her face to his. One hot tear trickled from the corner of her eye and ran down beside her nose. In an instant, Galen had put down his briefcase and folded her into his arms.

"Poor baby," he said, patting her back comfortingly. "What's wrong? Is there anything else you need to talk about? I don't have to rush off."

"N-no," Maggie said against his shoulder. Just the fact that she loved him and he'd given her one more blow she didn't need. She pulled her head back. "Should we be doing this on the sidewalk?" she asked in an attempt at humor.

"As far as I know, it isn't illegal," Galen said with a smile. "Are you sure?"

"It's just...everything," she said, sniffing back her tears and trying to smile at him. "I'm okay."

"No, you're not," Galen said, his gray eyes dark with worry as he looked at her intently. "Damn, I wish I could be more help to you right now, but...I'll see what I can do. I can't talk to Bruce, but I may be able to use some other people as go-betweens."

"Oh, Galen, thank you, but you've got too much to do already," Maggie protested. "There are a lot of people who need your help more than I do."

"No, there aren't," Galen said firmly. "If you're troubled, I'm troubled. Now keep your chin up and try to take one day at a time. All right?"

Maggie nodded and gave him a wavering smile. "Thanks again," she said.

"You're more than welcome," Galen replied. He gave her a little hug, then released her and picked up his briefcase again. "Give my love to your parents," he said, "and try not to worry." With that, he turned and walked away.

"I'll try," Maggie murmured, watching him go with a lump that felt as big as a soccer ball in her throat. Would he mind if she stole a little of the love he was sending to her parents, she wondered?

CHAPTER SEVEN

THE REST OF THE WEEK in Spring Mountain dragged by. The weather was sunny and Maggie took long hikes in the mountains, telling her parents she had to lose the weight she'd gained or the photographers would be furious with her. The truth was that she wanted to be alone in a tranquil setting, where she could try to reach some kind of compromise with herself about Galen, as well as mull over what she might do to cope with whatever surprise Bruce eventually sprang on them all.

But try as she might, neither project bore fruit. She knew Galen accepted her as a friend, the Maggie Preston he once had known, but it was not the role she wanted. And she knew her parents would be crushed no matter what form Bruce's straying from the straight and narrow might take. Her hope, a frail one, was that he had done nothing really wrong and was blowing something minor out of all proportion. The only things she was really sure about were that, no matter what happened, she was not going to marry Roger and she was going to retire from modeling very soon. What she might do then, if Galen wouldn't have her for his wife, she wasn't sure. Perhaps she might go to law school. Maybe he could at least use a partner.

Roger finally called on Friday night and seemed quite annoyed when Maggie refused his offer to send a company plane to pick her up on Sunday.

"You're going to have to get used to those little nice-ties," he said.

Maggie was tempted to tell him right then and there that she was not, but decided against it. Something that serious had to be done face-to-face. "I'm not going to waste a perfectly good plane ticket," she said instead. "Everything's all arranged, and Mom and Dad are taking me to the airport so I don't have to take that awful bus to Beckley. Don't fuss at me. I'm not in the mood for it."

"You must have had a rotten time there," Roger commented dryly.

"On the contrary," Maggie said, trying not to sound too unpleasant, "I've had a wonderful time. I don't want to leave."

"Mmm. No place like home, I guess," Roger said. "Well, I'll meet you at the airport, then, darling. I've missed you."

"Oops! There's the timer on the stove. I'll see you Sunday," Maggie said, and quickly hung up, smiling grimly. At least she'd managed to dodge telling Roger that she'd missed him, too, when she hadn't.

"What timer?" her mother asked, frowning.

"The one in my head," Maggie replied. "I had to end the conversation." She gave her mother a quick kiss on the cheek. "I think I'll go to bed now. All that hiking around is wearing me out." That was one benefit of the hikes she appreciated. She had managed to tire herself out enough to be able to sleep quite well.

When Maggie said goodbye to her parents on Sunday, they looked so sad that she longed to tell them she would be back in West Virginia to stay before long. But she was afraid her mother might tell Bruce, and he might pass the word to Roger before she had a chance to talk to him.

During the flight to New York she tried to brace herself for Roger's sure-to-be-enthusiastic welcome, but found it impossible to think of the perfect way to greet him without being either too warm or too cold. She would have to play it by ear and hope she was inspired at the right time. She entered the lounge at her gate, full of trepidation, but the only person she recognized was Roger's chauffeur, Silverton.

"Some trouble overseas," Silverton explained. "I believe he's in Germany. He expects to be back tomorrow."

Which was, Maggie mused wryly, the first she knew of any interests Roger had in that country. How had she managed to remain so completely ignorant about his business life? She had been busy herself, but that was really no excuse. She should have made it her business to know.

Very late that evening Roger called, full of apologies for not having met her plane. "It's morning here now," he said, "and I'll be flying back to you soon. It's been a rotten trip, and it will feel so good to hold you in my arms again. You can meet my plane, can't you?"

"Yes, I'll meet it. Of course," Maggie replied.

Her heart sank. She couldn't hit Roger with her news when he was down. In spite of everything, she owed him that much. He was warm and witty and charming, and had been very good to her. Of course, where those less fortunate were involved he had been unbelievably callous, and he had apparently made a perfect hell of her only brother's life. Oh, Lord, what a tangled web it was!

One look at Roger's tired face when she met his plane on Monday afternoon and Maggie's sympathetic heart went out to him. "I'm sorry you had such a bad time of it," she said when they were settled into the backseat of his limousine. "Tell me what went wrong."

Roger shook his head. "I don't want to talk about it." He kissed her hand lingeringly and smiled at her. "Tell me about your holiday instead. It must have been much more pleasant."

While she told him about going hiking and riding with an "old friend" and attending Bruce's "fabulous" party, the back of her mind was thinking that it was no wonder she knew so little about Roger's work. He refused to talk about it. Still, as she got into her routine in the next few days, and began enjoying the luxuries of her beautiful brownstone and the attentions of her housekeeper, Anna, who adored Maggie and waited on her as if she were royalty, she wondered if she would be making a mistake to give it all up. Life with Roger might not be perfect, but how rewarding would a different life be? It could be sheer frustration if Galen did not want her to be more than a friend. Could she really have the devotion he did to causes that so often seemed lost before they were begun? Did her principles really go that deep, or had Galen been right when he warned her not to make any quick decisions, his intuition telling him that she might vacillate once she was away from his influence? She was deeply troubled until one afternoon, the answer came from an unexpected quarter.

Maggie arrived home in a spring downpour and was drenched by the time she got from the taxi to her front door. To top it off, she had forgotten her key and Anna did not immediately answer her ring. She was about to speak sharply to her when she noticed that Anna's eyes were red and she was wringing her hands anxiously.

"What's the matter, Anna?" Maggie asked, immediately dropping her raincoat and umbrella on the floor and taking the tiny Jamaican woman into her arms.

"It's Silverton, Miss Maggie," Anna sobbed. "Mr. Roger, he fired him today."

"Oh, Anna, I'm so sorry," Maggie said sympathetically. She knew that Silverton, Roger's personal servant and chauffeur, a widower with a son in college, had fallen in love with Anna and the two were planning to be married.

"Would you come and talk to him?" Anna pleaded. "He's in the kitchen. He's so sad. And so angry."

"Of course," Maggie said, putting her arm around Anna and going along with her, wondering what had possessed Roger to fire the man. As far as she could tell, Silverton was devoted to Roger and his work had been flawless. It took her only a few minutes to find out the story. Roger had seen Silverton, a big husky man who was easy to spot, in a television news closeup about a group from Silverton's church who were organizing to protest what they felt were some recent abuses of their hard-won civil rights.

"He said that no servant of his was going to be a political rabble-rouser," Silverton said, his usually gentle face hard with anger. "It's not right, Miss Maggie. It's not American."

"It certainly isn't," Maggie agreed, her mind working rapidly, her temper roused in sympathy. The man ought to sue, but it would probably be his word against Roger's. Roger was too smart to let anyone else know something like that. "I don't suppose there were any witnesses to your firing?"

"Oh, yes, ma'am. He called Frenchie and Bernice to hear, so they'd know not to do anything like that. Called me an example.'' Silverton shook his huge head. "Now how's my Joseph going to finish college? I can find work, but it won't pay like Mr. Roger did. He won't give me good references.''

"Sue him,'' Maggie said, so angry she wished she were as big as Silverton and could give Roger the punishment he so richly deserved. "You'd win if Frenchie and Bernice would testify to what they heard. I think they could probably be subpoenaed to do it, but I don't know enough about the law to be sure. Of course, he'd probably fire them, too, if they did.''

"They're on borrowed time, anyway,'' Silverton said glumly. "They're in the same group I'm in, only Mr. Roger doesn't know it yet. They told me they aren't going to quit us just because of what he said, no matter what. But I can't afford a lawyer. I've got to keep every penny for Joseph's tuition.''

Maggie bit her lip. If only she could talk to Galen. She didn't know if he was licensed to practice law in New York, but he might know someone there who'd take Silverton's case for a nominal fee. Her eyes fell on the wall clock. It was only four. Galen might still be in his office, and she doubted he'd worry about that line being bugged.

"Hang on,'' she told Silverton. "I'm going to find you a good lawyer, cheap, and don't worry about Joseph's tuition. I'll pay it if necessary. I'm going to my room and phone. Don't go away.''

"Miss Maggie, I can't let you…'' Silverton began, but Maggie silenced him with a wave of her hand.

"Yes, you can. This is very important to me, maybe even more than it is to you.''

Maggie flew up the stairs, every doubt she'd had suddenly gone. She couldn't let people like Silverton go on being victimized by the Roger Balfours of the world. Not while she could do something about it.

She reached Galen, who was surprised as usual to hear from her, and quickly told him what she wanted and why. As she had hoped, he did have a friend in New York he was sure would help Silverton.

After Maggie had thanked him, Galen said, "You don't plan to tell Roger what you've done, do you?"

"Why, yes," Maggie said, frowning. "Why?"

"Don't. He could make life very unpleasant for your friends," Galen replied. "It wouldn't be the first time he's tried to intimidate a witness."

"Oh, I see. Okay, mum's the word. But I'd like to beat him over the head with something large and heavy," Maggie said.

Galen chuckled. "I'll pretend I didn't hear that if he asks me. I'm glad you called me. I hope everything works out for Silverton. He's lucky to have you for a friend."

There was a soft note in Galen's voice that made Maggie's heart give a hopeful skip. As she hurried downstairs to talk to Silverton, another thought struck her and she started to laugh. If Galen was as smart as she thought he was, he must have caught the clue that she was not going to marry Roger. Would that be enough to give him second thoughts?

That evening, Maggie was scheduled to go to a party with Roger at the home of some corporate executive. It was, she decided, time to gather her courage and tell him she would not marry him. When he'd called to invite her he'd mentioned that they needed to set a date to look at engagement rings. At the time she had murmured something noncommittal about thinking it over. Now she could tell him honestly that she had thought it over carefully and decided they shouldn't get married. It was a relief to have the decision firmly made, but she agonized until the last minute. Roger would be hurt, she knew, and in spite of everything she hated to hurt him.

Just before Roger was to arrive, Maggie put on a plain black dress that she thought was rather symbolic of what she was about to do. Then she gathered up all the jewelry he had given her and put it into a velvet bag and went downstairs. She set the velvet bag on the coffee table in her living room and stood beside it, massaging her icy fingertips and watching the door as if it could tell her when Roger would appear. When the bell rang, she answered the door quickly.

"Hello, Roger," she said, turning her face so that his kiss would find her cheek rather than her lips. "Come on in. I need to talk to you." She took his hand and led him to sit down on the sofa beside her.

"Is something wrong?" Roger asked, looking at her curiously. "Are you ill? That's not quite the dress I expected you to wear tonight."

"No, Roger, I'm not ill," Maggie said slowly. "I'm fine. But I'm afraid I have reached a decision that ... I should have made a long time ago. There's no easy way to say this, so I won't beat around the bush. I've been doing a lot of thinking lately, and I've decided that, in spite of the fact I'm very fond of you, I can't marry you."

Roger stared at her, his expression a mixture of shock and disbelief. "You can't mean that," he said.

Maggie put her hand over his and patted it comfortingly. "I know it's a surprise," she said, her voice quavering. "I tried to think of some way to make it easier for both of us, but there wasn't any. Yes, I really do mean it."

"Something happened while you were in West Virginia," Roger said, his eyes narrowing. "I've felt it since you got back. Did you meet someone else? Is that it?"

"No, Roger, that isn't it," Maggie said, hoping her expression didn't give her lie away. "I don't want to keep modeling much longer. I want to do something more meaningful. And when and if I do marry, it will be to someone who makes me a part of everything in his life. I'd never be happy being just an ornament in yours."

At first, Roger angrily expressed his doubts that she seriously thought her glamorous life was not rewarding enough. Then he turned charming, pleading that he adored her, that he needed someone lovely and sweet to distract him from his business problems, not become involved in them. "Besides," he added, "it's very complicated and quite boring to someone who isn't familiar with the details."

"Not if they're intelligent and curious," Maggie replied, trying hard to proceed calmly in spite of her increasing tension. She did not want to get trapped into blurting out something about either Galen or Silverton.

"Just what is it you're so curious about?" Roger demanded suspiciously.

Maggie shrugged. "For one thing, Bruce mentioned that you've been having trouble with some environmentalists in West Virginia. You might have known I'd be interested in that, considering my father's condition."

"Those people are a bunch of idealistic fools," Roger snapped, suddenly getting stiffly to his feet and glaring at her. "I'd done everything that's legally required to make my plant clean. If I did any more, I'd be out of business, thousands would be out of work, and the economy of West Virginia would be worse off than it is. Those damned environmentalists need to learn some basic facts. A certain amount of pollution is unavoidable, and it's necessary if you want to turn a profit and stay in business."

The image of little Carrie Bryant suddenly came to Maggie's mind. "What about the toxic-waste dump that polluted the streams and groundwater?" she asked quietly. "Was that necessary?"

Roger glared at her. "You sound exactly like that sleazy environmental lawyer from down there in the sticks. Galen Kendrick." He spat the name out contemptuously. "That bastard's nothing but a damned troublemaker." He added several more profane comments on Galen's competence and character while Maggie stared at him openmouthed. Roger seldom swore. For a man for whom Roger expressed such contempt, Galen had certainly gotten under his skin, doubtless because he was in the right. She felt like telling Roger exactly what she thought of his opinion, but held her tongue. It wouldn't help either her or Galen.

She shrugged. "I don't know about that," she said, "but it doesn't matter. I can't marry you. I hope we can still be friends."

Roger paced around the room a few times then shook his head. "I'm not going to take that no for a final answer, Maggie," he said, coming to a halt in front of her. "I think your trip home has gotten you off on some kind of temporary track that you'll get over, and when you do you'll see that you'd have the best possible life with me. Think about it a while longer."

Maggie shook her head. She picked up the bag of jewels and stood up. "No, Roger," she said firmly, "I'm not going to do that. My answer is final. Here." She held the bag out to him. "I don't think I should keep these expensive jewels. It wouldn't be fair to you."

Roger brushed her hand away, glaring at her. "Keep them," he roared, his voice several decibels louder than Maggie had ever heard it. "Your answer is *not* final. I won't accept it."

Maggie's temper finally gave way. "I'm afraid you're going to have to," she said, her own voice rising. She stuffed the bag into Roger's coat pocket. "I wanted to keep this pleasant, but since you won't let me, I won't. I don't want to be your friend. I don't ever want to see you again. Now get out!" With that she marched over to the door, jerked it open and pointed. "Now!"

As Roger reached the door, he paused and stared at Maggie intently through icy blue eyes whose deadly chill was completely at odds with the smile that curved his lips. "You're being a fool, Maggie," he said in a liquid voice like steel. "I hope for your sake your brother can talk some sense into you."

"Don't count on it," Maggie snapped.

After she had shut the door behind him with a bang, Maggie shuddered. The vicious look on Roger's face had been something she had never seen before, a glimpse at a stranger she didn't want to know. What if she had married him? Would that man have surfaced to make her life as tortured as Bruce's? She still wasn't sure where Bruce fit into the puzzle, but it was now much easier to believe that Roger was capable of doing anything to get what he wanted. Well, whatever he might think to the contrary, she was not going to have more to do with him. She'd probably better warn Bruce that he might expect an appeal from Roger.

Maggie braced herself for a tirade from Bruce when she called him, but to her surprise he sounded quite calm.

"Don't worry about it, Maggie," he told her. "I think I can handle it." He paused and then said hesitantly, "You're in love with Galen, aren't you?"

It was Maggie's turn to hesitate. Should she tell Bruce the truth? It couldn't help matters if he passed that to Roger. "Well, uh, I . . . I do like him a lot," she said finally. To her surprise, Bruce laughed softly.

"Don't beat around the bush, sis," he said. "It's plain as the nose on your face that you do, and you don't need to worry about my making life difficult for you. There is one thing that I'd like for you to do, though. It's very important. I'm going to have to string along with Roger when he asks me to talk to you. I need more time to get myself organized for the . . . inevitable. So it will help a lot if you could pretend for a while, too, that you're really thinking over what I've said. Can you do that? I'll let you know as soon as you can drop the pretense."

"All right," Maggie agreed, baffled but relieved by Bruce's reformed attitude. Could Galen have talked to him, after all? "Is there anything else I can do to help you?"

"Not a thing," Bruce replied. "Just take good care of yourself. I love you."

"I love you, too," Maggie said. She hung up, feeling dazed but happy. At least one of her worst worries seemed to have evaporated into thin air. She frowned. When she found out what Roger had done to Bruce to make him so frightened before, she was going to make him sorry he'd ever met her. Meanwhile, she had better start making plans to phase out her modeling career and get on to something different. After Silverton's experience, becoming a lawyer sounded even more appealing.

The next two weeks were what Maggie would readily have described as a nightmare. Everywhere she met opposition to her plans. Her agent was first distraught, then furious, then cajoling. "You'd go crazy back in West Virginia, sweetheart," he said. "It's practically primitive! Besides, you belong where the whole world can glory in your beauty."

To that, Maggie made an unladylike reply. "I might point out," she added coldly, "that I have made you a bundle, and it does seem that you could be helpful now when I ask it."

The agent's legal counsel hemmed and hawed and tried to make Maggie believe there was nothing she could do to break any of her longer-term contracts.

"If necessary," she snapped "I'll either get fat or have plastic surgery. Do something!"

At last the man confessed that a lot of loopholes had been written into some of them, "In case something better turned up."

After a week, Bruce called to say that Roger had contacted him. "He wants me to call him back and let him know if you've become more reasonable," he said. "Any ideas what I could tell him to stall him off?"

Maggie racked her brain. "I know, tell him that I was hysterical and insulting and hung up on you, but that I told you I'd be home next week and you'll get me straightened out then. I will be coming home, a week from tomorrow."

"Great idea," Bruce agreed.

IT WAS A MONTH TO THE DAY after Maggie had left West Virginia that she was finally able to leave New York once more. She would have to return in two weeks for one last round of spring fashion shows. At that time, she planned to put her brownstone on the market and thereafter return only to finish out any remaining obligations.

As the plane took Maggie homeward, she felt a mixture of happiness and pain. It felt good to know the direction her future would take, but she was less sure than ever about her chances with Galen. If it was plain to Bruce that she was in love with him, it surely must be to Galen, and he had taken pains to make a couple of remarks designed to let her know that he did not have marriage in mind. Somehow, she had to learn to accept him as a good friend, for he was involved in many of the things that were meaningful to her. She could learn so much from him. Until she could do that, she had better make sure they weren't alone together in any romantic spots. Galen might not be interested in marriage, but he did find her physically attractive, and it was only a matter of time before she would give in to him.

Men! she thought grimly. They never seemed to be anything but trouble for her. Maybe what she ought to do was go far away to get her law degree, then specialize in women's rights issues. But she loved West Virginia and wanted to be near her father. She would just have to learn to be tougher.

Maggie had taken a flight into Charleston this time, expecting Bruce to meet her. She scanned the waiting crowd, but didn't see him, so she sat down to wait. She'd been sitting only a few moments when in the distance, above the rest of the crowd in the corridor, she saw a familiar head of black hair coming in her direction. Her heart gave a lurch, then started racing.

"Keep calm," she muttered to herself. Galen was probably coming to meet someone else. Bruce would show up soon, too. Even though her brother had said he wouldn't make trouble between her and Galen, she doubted their meeting would be more than barely civil at best. She watched Galen draw closer, his wide-set gray eyes darting from face to face in the crowd between them. Maggie pursed her mouth and sat motionless, longing to be able to go and throw herself into his arms, to be coming home to him. Then his eyes met hers, and she felt a jolt like lightning. He smiled, then wedged his way through a clump of people toward her.

"Sorry I'm late," he said, coming to stand in front of her. "I didn't know I was going to be picking you up until about a half hour ago." He bent his head and frowned as Maggie stared at him blankly. "Are you that disappointed to see me instead of Bruce?" he asked.

"Heavens, no!" Maggie said, getting quickly to her feet and giving him a bright smile. "I—I'm just...surprised." And about ready to jump out of her skin at the excitement the sight of Galen generated. He had apparently been too busy at home to bother shaving, and the shadow on his jaw gave him a darkly romantic look that was devastating to her efforts to control her emotions.

"How did you happen to come instead of Bruce?" she asked. Could the two of them actually be getting along all right now? "Did he call you? Is something wrong with him?"

Galen laughed. "No, but I gathered his car isn't well. He called your mother and she called me. Lucky she caught me. I was about to start for Spring Mountain when she called."

"Really?" Maggie said, eyeing him suspiciously. "You look to me as if you were hard at work."

Seeing Maggie's eyes on his chin, Galen put his hand up and felt it. "Damn. I forgot to shave, didn't I?" he grinned at Maggie. "I told you I was absentminded. Come on, let's go. It's a beautiful spring day. Much too nice to spend indoors. We'll go over to Haven Hill and go riding as soon as you've said hello to your parents and changed your clothes. I brought my riding clothes along.''

Alone with Galen. A romantic setting. Just what she didn't need, Maggie thought grimly. "I can't," she said, hurrying along beside him. "I'll have to unpack. I wouldn't want to keep you waiting that long.''

Galen looked at her, cocked an eyebrow and shook his head. "You don't have to unpack yet," he said in a voice that sounded, Maggie thought, as if he had no intention of arguing about the matter.

"But I still don't have any proper riding clothes,'' she said lamely.

"What you wore the last time will do just fine,'' Galen said. "Remember to get some the next time you go shopping.''

Maggie sighed. She would have to find some other excuse before they got to Spring Mountain. Her parents wouldn't be any help. They'd probably send her off on a world cruise alone with Galen if they thought it would promote something between them.

"How are things in New York?'' Galen asked as they drove along. "Did Silverton get in touch with the lawyer?''

"Yes, but I don't know if anything's happened yet,'' Maggie replied.

"You'll probably hear about that from Roger when it happens,'' Galen said dryly.

"I, uh, suppose so,'' Maggie said, feeling a sudden twinge of anxiety. She had forgotten that Galen didn't know for certain that she'd told Roger she wouldn't marry him. Since Bruce had asked her to keep that matter quiet for a while, she expected that she shouldn't tell

Galen yet, either. Not that it would make any difference to him, but still . . .

"How is Carrie getting along?" she asked to change the subject.

"Not well," Galen said, grimacing. "She's back in the hospital. There's almost no hope, but she's hanging on. She wants very much to see you again."

"Oh, we should have gone right there from the airport," Maggie said, stricken. "Poor little angel. I'll go and see her tomorrow."

Galen reached over and squeezed her hand. "Brace yourself, Maggie," he said. "We'll probably lose her."

Maggie looked at him and nodded, her eyes swimming with tears. "I understand," she said. She also knew that Galen understood how she felt, that both of them felt almost as heartbroken as if they were losing a child of their own. That depth of understanding was what made being with Galen so special. It made the bearing of any other kind of pain seem trivial.

During the rest of the drive, Maggie managed to steer the conversation away from her affairs in New York by reminiscing about the time she and Galen were youngsters in Spring Mountain. When they arrived at her parents' house, Galen immediately announced that he was going to steal her away to go riding, and she realized that she had completely forgotten to come up with a reasonable excuse. Maybe, she thought wryly as she went to change her clothes, subconsciously she hadn't really wanted to. She was going to have to watch herself.

Sheila Kendrick welcomed them with her usual enthusiasm, scolded Galen for not shaving, then shooed them off for their ride as soon as he had shaved and changed his clothes.

"Shall we try the Bald Knob ride again?" Galen asked when they were on their horses.

The thought of the beautiful lonely spot sent a wave of panic through Maggie's already tightly wound nerves. "Uh, why don't we try something new?" she asked, then felt her cheeks go warm as Galen gave her an amused, knowing smile.

"All right," he said. "I think I know another place that you'll like. Follow me." He urged his horse forward, and Maggie soon had to put Val into a canter to keep up.

Wherever he was going, he was in a terrible hurry to get there, Maggie thought, trying her best to sit her horse properly as they flew across the northern pastures of Haven Hill. At the very end of the field, she abandoned all pretense, for Galen took his horse in a jump over a small creek and Val followed, with Maggie clinging desperately to her neck.

"Don't you dare do that again without warning me!" Maggie shouted angrily.

Galen wheeled his horse around and trotted beside her, grinning mischievously. "Fun, wasn't it?" he said, his eyes flashing with laughing silver lights.

"Not exactly," Maggie grumbled. "I nearly fell off. Where on earth are we going?"

"Up there," Galen replied, pointing skyward. "Observatory Hill. I named it that when I was a kid. Dad and I used to take a telescope up there and look at the stars. We cleared out a few trees and used the logs to make some rough benches to sit on. I haven't been up there in a while, but the view is even better than the one from Bald Knob. Come on." He made a motion like a cavalry captain leading a charge as he wheeled again and started off.

Maggie took a deep breath and followed, reminding herself over and over that she was going to be calm, cool and very collected. Even if it killed her, which she feared it might. She had been so absorbed in her own tension she had just noticed Galen was acting keyed up, too. Bossier than usual. And very eager to get where they were going.

They soon started upward, going more slowly on the steep trail. The spring woods were beautiful, the trees unfurling their leaves of brilliant green, splashes of wildflowers lighting the slopes with carpets of pink and white and delicate lavender.

"It will be even more beautiful when the rhododendrons bloom," Galen remarked.

"Yes, it will," Maggie agreed, but she doubted she would notice even if they were suddenly to pop into bloom right before her eyes. She was too busy trying not to look at Galen's broad shoulders, encased in a loose-fitting white shirt that, with his tight black riding pants and high black boots, made him look like a pirate. A very dangerous pirate.

When they reached the summit, Galen flung himself from his horse and reached for Val's reins. "Hop down," he said, smiling at Maggie. "I'll tie these fellows to a tree. We can sit down and soak up the sunshine and enjoy the view for a while."

Maggie lowered herself, standing stiffly in the middle of the small cleared area while Galen tied the horses. He removed his horse's saddle and brought his blanket with him as he limped to her side. He flipped the blanket out smooth on the ground then reached for Maggie's hand.

"Let's sit," he said, pulling her down beside him. Then he put his arm around her, tucked her against his shoulder and laid his cheek in her hair. "There now," he said, heaving a deep sigh, "isn't this better than un-packing?"

"Oh, yes," Maggie said, wishing that she didn't sound so breathless. Her heart was threatening to race out of control, and she was holding herself as rigid as she could against the violent urge of her body to simply melt into Galen like butter into hot toast. She should move away now, while she was still able. But was she able? She thought hard about moving, but nothing happened. She was caught, her will useless.

As if in a dream, she felt Galen rub his cheek against her hair, then put his other arm around her and pull her closer. She felt his head bending until his lips touched her cheek. She shivered and her face turned toward his. Luminous pools of gray met her eyes and beckoned with their magic. Soft lips lured her to taste their sweetness. Her lips parted. She was falling, falling, waiting for the moment when those lips touched hers.

And then they did. She gasped at the wonder of it, the shower of sparks that flew before her closed eyes like embers from a fire. Her arms stole around Galen and held him close, her fingers digging eagerly into his shoulders. Galen's tongue plundered her mouth, his hand moved beneath her sweater. A low sound of pleasure burst from Maggie's throat at the flood of desire that coursed through her. In response, Galen pressed her back against the blanket, then pulled her sweater off and tossed it aside. His hands grasped her shoulders, his lips found hers again, then slowly began a delicate journey downward, leaving a trail of whisper-light kisses. His fingers stroked her with a feathery touch that seemed to Maggie's senstitized skin to create electricity at every point of contact. She wanted him, oh, how she wanted him, she thought in a daze of longing.

Galen unfastened the button of Maggie's slacks and slid the zipper down. A deep guttural sound escaped from Maggie's throat.

"No!" she cried. She wrenched herself free of Galen's weight and sat up, grasping her knees, burying her face against them and shaking her head. "I can't," she sobbed, shaking her head.

"Maggie, what is it?" Galen asked, his voice harsh with frustration.

"I don't want to," she gasped, raising her tear-stained face to look at him. He looked bewildered. "I...I don't...I don't know what I want," she said. "It's just not...I'm not ready. I'm not sure...I'm sorry." She lunged to the side and grabbed her sweater. She pulled it on with frantic fingers and scrambled to her feet. "I shouldn't have come here," she said. "I knew what you'd want. It was a mistake. I won't do it again."

Galen's face darkened. "Damn it, Maggie, you wanted it, too," he growled. "What kind of ridiculous game is this? It's not like you."

"I'm still too confused," Maggie said, shaking her head. "I don't know what I want." Dear Lord, how could she lie like that? The hurt and anger in Galen's eyes was terrible to see. "I'd better go home now," she said, and turned and fled to her horse.

The ride down the mountain and then the drive home from Haven Hill were sheer torture. Galen was silent, his jaw set in an uncompromising line. Whenever Maggie stole a glance at him, she could see the muscles in his cheeks working, as if, she thought, he were contemplating chewing her up and spitting her out in little bits. He refused her strained invitation to come in to her parents' house with a curt, "No, thanks," scarcely giving Maggie time to shut the car door before he drove away.

"Isn't Galen coming in?" her mother asked the moment she opened the door.

"No. He's busy," Maggie replied, brushing past her hurriedly so that she wouldn't see the tears in her eyes. "I'm going to unpack," she called over her shoulder. She went into her room, shut the door behind her and sat down on the bed, her hands clenched. This was not going to do. She couldn't go on like this.

CHAPTER EIGHT

THE LONG NIGHT brought Maggie no sleep, but it did provide her with plenty of time to think. No matter what direction her thoughts took she always arrived at the same place. She had to talk things out with Galen, tell him of her recent decisions and go on from there. There would be no more lies. And, if the talk should get that far, she would tell him that while she preferred marriage, if he wanted her in some other relationship, that was all right with her. One fact was crystal clear in her mind. She couldn't live without him.

In the morning, Maggie dressed in a colorful turquoise print skirt and top, and added dangling earrings and a necklace with tiny carved elephants in the middle. She wanted her outfit to be bright and cheerful, something Carrie would like.

"I'm going to the hospital to see Carrie Bryant first," she told her parents, "and then I'm going to see Galen. I don't know when I'll be home, so for heaven's sake, don't worry. And don't call Bruce!"

"I'll see that she doesn't," her father said with a meaningful look at her mother.

On the way to the hospital, Maggie stopped at a toy store. The sight of all of the beautiful toys saddened her. There were so many things Carrie would never get to enjoy. At last, she chose a soft brown bear who looked so lovable and cuddly Maggie was tempted to buy one for herself. It had been so long, she mused, since she'd had anything like that. Wouldn't it be fun to have children so she had an excuse to buy it?

Maggie found Carrie in bed in a large sunny room with another little girl who had cancer. John and Susan Bryant were there, and Susan was playing cards with her daughter. As soon as Carrie saw Maggie, her face lit up.

"I knew you'd come to see me," she said pushing herself up and holding out her arms to Maggie.

"Hello, love," Maggie said, holding the frail little body close and blinking back her tears. "Of course I came to see you. And I brought a little friend for you to hug. I think he needs someone like you to love him." She took the bear from the bag and handed it to Carrie.

"Oh, he does," Carrie said, crushing him against her cheek. "Thank you, Maggie. He's so soft. Galen brought me a soft bunny once, but one of the boys left him outside and the goat ate it." Carrie giggled irrepressibly, and Maggie laughed, marveling at the child's ability to stay so cheerful. Carrie invited her to try to beat her at concentration, and Maggie was losing badly when they were interrupted by the arrival of Carrie's doctor.

"Saved from a trouncing by a higher authority," Maggie said, getting up and shaking hands with the man, who was introduced to her as Dr. Grant. She watched closely as the doctor checked Carrie's charts and talked to her for a few minutes. He was a balding middle-aged man, and in his tired, lined face she could see that no matter how long he had dealt with cases like Carrie's, they still touched him deeply. When he left, she followed him into the hall.

"Could you tell me how things are going for Carrie?" she asked. "I'm a friend of Galen Kendrick's."

The doctor shook his head. "Frankly we need a miracle," he said. He looked at Maggie curiously. "Don't I recognize you?"

"Perhaps," Maggie replied evasively. "Has absolutely everything been done for her that could be? I don't mean to imply that you wouldn't, but is there anything available, anywhere, that could be tried?"

Dr. Grant smiled. "You're the model! I think your face is on my coffee table at home. My wife subscribes to all of those women's magazines."

"That's me," Maggie said with a sigh. "About Carrie..."

The doctor rubbed his forehead. "There is one new experimental treatment, a result of some recent breakthroughs in biotechnology. It's a long shot, but there have been some rather exciting results. The problem is that Carrie would have to go to the hospital in Pennsylvania where they're doing the experimental work. If they would accept her in the program, most of her expenses would be covered by a government grant, but her parents wouldn't be able to afford to go along, and they refuse to ask Galen for any more help. He said he'd be glad to pay their way, but..." The doctor shrugged. "I can't force them to do it."

"Maybe they'll let me help," Maggie said. "If they will, do you think Carrie would be accepted?"

"I believe so." Dr. Grant grinned. "I know the man in charge very well. He's my son."

"I'll see what I can do," Maggie said.

"Let me know immediately if you succeed," the doctor said seriously. "We haven't much time."

"I will," Maggie promised. She bit her lip and turned toward Carrie's room. How could she persuade the Bryants to accept her help? They barely knew her.

Suddenly an idea came to her and she smiled. She went into the room, played another game with Carrie, then invited John and Susan to come to the lounge with her. There, she told them that Dr. Grant had mentioned the experimental treatment to her, along with their reluctance to accept more money from Galen. Then she sprang her idea on them. "I have a foundation," she said, "that pays the expenses for families who need financial help to accompany their children to treatment centers away from their home. We can also help with paying for care for the other children, if they can't go with you. If you'd like for Carrie to try the treatment, we'd be happy to help you."

The looks on the Bryants' faces as they turned toward each other was, Maggie thought, enough reward to last her a lifetime. Within the hour, they were making arrangements with Dr. Grant for Carrie's trip.

Maggie returned to her car a short time later, feeling buoyantly happy, but a little dazed. How on earth did one go about setting up a foundation? She needed a lawyer. And, she realized suddenly, she knew just where to find one.

She arrived at Galen's offices a little after one o'clock.

"I'm terribly sorry, Miss Preston," said his secretary, "but you've just missed him. He's going to be in court all afternoon, I'm afraid."

"Darn," Maggie said, frowning. "Will he be coming back here when he's through?"

"I doubt it. Do you want to leave a message for him to call you if he does?"

"No, I'll catch him later," Maggie replied. She returned to her car, feeling terribly let down. She had been so eager to see Galen today. Well, she would. She'd go to his house late in the afternoon and wait for him, if it took all night. Meanwhile, she might as well go shopping.

It was almost five o'clock when Maggie drove to Galen's house. His car was not in the driveway, and as soon as she got out of her car, Betsy came bounding across the lawn, barking loudly, followed by four fat, rollicking little balls of black fur on legs. The puppies were adorable, but Maggie wondered if Betsy was still defending them fiercely from intruders.

"Remember me?" Maggie asked, holding her hand across the gate toward Betsy. "Woof," said Betsy, and then began to lick her hand and wag her tail. Relieved, Maggie let herself in through the gate and closed it carefully behind her. She went to sit on the side porch, the puppies following along and nipping at her ankles, then tumbling over each other as they tried to climb onto her lap. She picked each one up and cuddled it, while Betsy watched approvingly, seeming to take Maggie's compliments on her fine family as only her due.

When it was nearly six and Galen had still not returned, Maggie began to worry that he had decided to go out for dinner. She had brought along some groceries in hopes that he would let her cook dinner for him. She went up the steps and tried the door. Locked. Well, she hadn't thought he'd leave it open.

Suddenly she had an idea. People on TV were always opening doors with credit cards. This lock didn't look very new, and there was no dead bolt that she could see. Quickly she took a card from her billfold. How would that work? Slide it in, pry back a little, and . . .

"How about that?" Maggie said, smiling as the door opened. "My life of crime begins."

She carried her bag of groceries into Galen's kitchen and set it on the counter, turned on the lights and began putting the perishables away in the refrigerator. She had just finished when she heard a car come into the drive, followed by the sound of Galen's voice greeting Betsy and the pups. She heard his footsteps on the stairs. Her heart began to pound, and she held on to the counter for support. The door flew open and Galen flung his briefcase across the floor, where it crashed to a stop against the wall. He closed the door behind him with a bang and leaned against it, looking down, his face fiercely angry.

Maggie swallowed, terror sending icy tentacles around her heart. Galen must have seen her car out in front, and he was absolutely livid with anger. Slowly he raised his head. His expression changed to shocked surprise.

"Maggie! My God, what are you doing here?" he demanded.

A rush of relief made Maggie's knees weak. He hadn't known she was here at all. "Is that the only way you know how to say hello?" she asked.

Galen ran his fingers through his already disorderly hair and shook his head. "No, but—" he gestured to the door "—I thought I locked the door. If I'm starting to forget things like that—"

"You didn't forget," Maggie assured him quickly. "I'm guilty of breaking and entering with a credit card. You do need better locks, I'm afraid."

"I guess so." Galen limped slowly to the table and sank into a chair. "I could use a drink," he said. "How about you?"

"Well, uh, sure," Maggie replied. This wasn't quite the way she'd planned this meeting, anticipating that Galen would still be angry with her. Apparently something had happened to him today that overshadowed his anger at her so much that he had forgotten it, at least temporarily. Even his surprise at seeing her did not last for long. "What do you want and where is it?" she asked. "I'll play bartender."

"The cabinet above the refrigerator," Galen replied. "Scotch on the rocks."

Maggie poured Galen a stiff drink and made herself a very watery one. "Thank you," he said, attempting a smile as she put his drink in front of him. He took a sip, then gazed at her as she sat down around the corner of the table from him. "You look very pretty today," he said. "Did you go to see Carrie?"

"Yes." Maggie nodded. "In fact, that's one of the reasons I'm here. I need a good lawyer." When Galen raised his eyebrows questioningly and took another sip of Scotch, she went on to explain what she had done.

When she had finished, Galen shook his head. "You continually amaze me, Maggie," he said. "After yesterday, I wasn't sure what to expect of you."

"I know," Maggie said, her cheeks flushing as she looked away from Galen's gaze. "That's another reason I'm here. But what about the foundation? Is that going to be hard to set up? I'll need to give the Bryants money right away."

"We'll work it out as quickly as possible," Galen replied, "but it could be fairly complicated. I'm not an expert in that kind of law, but I know who to contact. Meanwhile, you need to think about exactly what charitable works you'll fund and how much money you want to put into it. You'll need a staff to administer it, also. Unless you plan to do it yourself."

Maggie's eyes brightened. "Why, yes. I might do that. I'll probably need help, but I think I will! After I sell my brownstone I'll have a couple of million net, and I can put my stocks into it, too. And I can go around and raise funds. It will have to be nonprofit and tax-deductible, won't it? How does that work?'' She stopped, suddenly aware that Galen was staring at her. ''What is it?'' she asked.

''Are you really thinking about selling your brownstone?'' he asked.

''Not just thinking about it,'' Maggie replied, glad that the conversation had taken a turn that allowed her to explain her recent decisions to Galen. ''I lied to you yesterday,'' she said. ''I'm not confused about anything anymore. Not at all.''

She went on to tell him everything that had happened, including Bruce's plea that she play along for a while with Roger's persistent quest. ''That's my only excuse for lying to you,'' she said, ''and it isn't a very good one. I should have told you. I don't know what Bruce is up to, but he'd better get it straightened out in a hurry, because I want Roger out of my life, period.''

''I can understand that,'' Galen said, staring at his glass while he swished the ice cubes around in it. ''I'd give Bruce a little longer, though. It sounds as if he's really trying to work out his problem.''

Maggie sighed. ''I will. Anyway, that's the rest of what I came to tell you, but I also brought along some steaks and mushrooms, if you'd like me to cook dinner for you. You look awfully tired.''

''I am,'' Galen replied. ''Steak sounds good. While you work on that, I'll have another drink and read the newspaper.''

Galen poured himself another half drink and went into the living room, leaving Maggie alone in the kitchen. It was, she thought with a smile, what being married to him would be like. Rather than bother him with questions, she hunted around until she found the pans and dishes she needed, and within an hour had the dinner on the table and called Galen to come and eat.

"Very good," he said, sampling the steak immediately. He ate so hungrily, not saying a word, that Maggie suspected he had skipped lunch. From his haggard look, she wondered if he had even slept the night before. She had almost forgotten that she hadn't.

"You look exhausted," she said when he'd finished. "If you like, I'll just clean up the kitchen and then go on home so you can go to bed."

Galen turned his gray eyes on Maggie and studied her intently. "Maggie," he said, "I am tired, and I'm often quiet. Especially when I've just lost a case. If I'm boring you, go home by all means."

Maggie felt as if a glass of ice water had just been thrown in her face. "Oh, Galen," she whispered, "I'm so sorry. How very, very thoughtless of me. Here I've been chattering away about all kinds of things when you have something like that on your mind." She gave him a shaky smile. "It never occurred to me that you ever lost a case."

"I never plan to, but it happens," Galen said, responding with a fleeting smile of his own.

"Want to talk about it?" Maggie asked timidly.

"Not right now," Galen said, shaking his head. "Not until I've finished cursing myself for everything I did wrong." He stood up and stretched, then groaned. "Right now, I think I'll take a hot shower and then lie down on my bed and watch something dumb on the television in my room for a while. You can come along if you want. There's a comfortable chair up there. Or go home if you'd prefer. I'm not apt to be very good company tonight."

"I'll come along," Maggie said quickly, "as soon as I clean up the kitchen." After all, the words "for better or for worse" were part of the marriage ceremony, and if she wanted Galen to think along those lines someday, she didn't want him to feel she was incapable of dealing with something as simple as his being tired and depressed. Besides, maybe she could find some way to cheer him up.

Maggie was used to cleaning up as she went along, and it didn't take her long to wash the remaining dishes. She was about to start for the stairs when Galen called down to her.

"Bring me up a glass of water and the aspirin, will you please, Maggie? The aspirin are in the cabinet above the sink."

"Coming right up," she answered. Poor dear, he must have a terrible headache. She made a pitcher of ice water and carried it, along with the glass and medicine, upstairs on a tray.

Galen was already in his bed, a big old-fashioned four-poster with a thick soft quilt in a lively shade of periwinkle blue that was tucked across his bare chest and under his arms. He had several pillows propping him so that he could see the television, but he appeared to be staring into space rather than paying attention to the program.

Seeing Galen lying there looking so tired and vulnerable made Maggie long to be able to hold him and comfort him, and the sight of his broad bare shoulders and the curly black hair on his chest made her tingle from head to foot. Was he wearing anything at all? Steady, Maggie, she warned herself as she carried the tray to his bedside.

"Here you are, sir," she said a little breathlessly. "Bad headache?" The ice tinkled as she set the tray on the nightstand next to Galen, poured out a glass of water and handed him the aspirin bottle.

"Thank you," Galen said, nodding in response to her question. "I feel as if someone's hammering on my head and they tied a knot in the back of my neck." While Maggie watched he dropped several aspirin into his hand, then swallowed them all with one large gulp of water. "There," he said, handing her the glass and grimacing in pain as he rubbed the back of his neck. "Maybe that will help."

"Poor baby," Maggie said sympathetically, then blushed scarlet at the quick look he gave her.

"Baby?" he said, cocking one black eyebrow at her.

"It was just a figure of speech," she said tightly. "You've called me that, I recall, and I used to say that to Bruce when he was sick or hurt." She made a face at Galen. "He didn't like it much, either."

Galen gave Maggie an amused smile. "It didn't sound that bad," he said.

Encouraged, Maggie ventured, "If you'd like, I could massage your neck and shoulders for you. I used to do that when Bruce had gotten his all kinked up from chopping wood or something. He said it helped a lot."

"All right," Galen said, after a few moments during which he stared blankly at the television screen. A commercial with a big bunch of teenagers leaping wildly around, showing toothy smiles and perfectly tanned bodies to advertise a soft drink, was playing. "I hate that commercial," he growled, pushing some of his pillows aside and turning onto his stomach, his face away from her. "It makes me tired just watching it."

Maggie chuckled. "I can see why your secretary calls you a grouch," she said, kneeling on the bed beside him. "Just relax now."

She took hold of Galen's shoulders near his neck and began to work the muscles with a kneading motion. The muscles were as hard and tight as steel, but his skin was warm and smooth, the sensation that it communicated to Maggie's hands making her painfully aware that while she might be able to get Galen's muscles to relax, she was not going to have any such luck for herself. Being able to touch him, caress him, to grasp those massive shoulders, sent rivers of longing coursing through her. She wanted to lay her cheek against him, to kiss her way across his back and into the place where the dark hair curled slightly at the nape of his neck after his shower. Instead, she slowly worked her way back and forth, then up and down, her thumbs pressing against his spine. Several times Galen made little sounds of pleasure, and she wondered if it was only the relief from pain that he enjoyed, or if he felt the same current flowing between them that she did.

Gradually Maggie felt softness replace the hard tension. Galen made no more sounds, and his breathing became quiet and regular. He was asleep. Carefully Maggie lifted her hands, wishing wistfully that someday she would see that pair of shoulders every night beside her. She started to pull the covers over him, then stopped. She bent her head and softly kissed his shoulder. "I love you, Galen," she whispered, then finished covering him.

Maggie turned and sat down, trying to move slowly and not shake the bed. She thought briefly of going to sit in the big soft lounge chair, but quickly decided not to. Instead, she leaned back against the extra pillows

Galen had pushed aside and took a deep shaky breath as she looked at his dark head on the pillow beside her. It wasn't exactly being in bed with him, but it was the next best thing. Feeling warm and contented, she closed her eyes and was soon fast asleep. She awakened with a start when the telephone on the nightstand beside her rang.

"Hello?" she said, managing to grab it after the first ring. There was a click, then the dial tone returned. At the same moment, she felt Galen's arm fall heavily across her.

"Who was it?" he asked, turning his head and staring at her vaguely through sleepy, partly opened eyes.

"I don't know. They hung up," Maggie replied. "Probably a wrong number."

Galen's eyes opened wider. "You're still here," he said, pulling his arm back. "What time is it?" He raised himself and peered at the digital clock next to his telephone, then looked at Maggie again. "It's almost midnight. I didn't plan to sleep all evening."

"You were awfully tired," Maggie said, inhibiting an impulse to reach out and stroke his hair from his forehead. He still looked like a big sleepy bear. "How's your headache?"

"Gone. I think your massage knocked me out completely." He was beginning to look more alert and he studied Maggie curiously. "Were you planning to stay all night?" he asked.

Maggie suddenly felt dizzy, in spite of the fact that she was almost lying down. The huskiness of Galen's voice and the shafts of silver light glowing in the gray of his eyes sent a shiver through her. She reached out and caressed that irresistible lock of hair back from his forehead. "Would you like me to?" she asked.

A devilish spark flashed at her from deep in Galen's eyes, which were now very definitely awake. "Sit up a minute," he commanded. Maggie did so, wondering what he had in mind. She quickly found out, for he re-arranged the pillows, then put his arm around her and pulled her to his shoulder as he laid back against them.

"Tell me about your bedroom in New York," he said, delicately tracing the outline of her face with his finger-tips. "I've often tried to imagine what it was like."

"Y-you have?" Maggie stammered. Finding herself stretched out next to Galen in his arms, on his bed, with only the blanket between them, left her feeling totally disoriented, longing to snatch the blanket away and at the same time trembling with an irrational fear that it would be gone before she had the chance to say some of the other things to him that she wanted to.

"Uh-huh," Galen replied, touching her lips softly with his and then drawing back. "I've wondered if the walls were all gilded and mirrored, so that you could see yourself from every angle."

"Heavens, no!" Maggie cried. "Do you think I'm a narcissist? It's just a big airy room. The ceilings are high, because it's an old building. And the decorator was go-ing through his peach period or something, so every-thing is done in shades of peach."

"That sounds nice," Galen said, his eyes scanning Maggie's face, then resting on her lips. He touched her lips with his again. "How big is your house?"

"It's...uh...let's see." Maggie could scarcely think, her head was spinning so. Galen was playing some kind of game with her. What did he care how big her house was? What did it matter, anyway? "I don't remember," she said, frowning. "Galen, I want to talk to you about...something."

Galen shifted Maggie closer, put his other arm around her, then said, his lips against her forehead, "Oh? What?"

What? Oh, Lord, what was she going to say? Maggie tilted her head a little, then raised her hand to caress Galen's cheek and run an exploratory finger along one of his dark brows. She followed the bridge of Galen's nose to its end, then skipped her finger down to his lips and began to trace them. All the while, she could feel Galen watching her intently.

"About…us," she said finally, raising her eyes to his. "I want to know where we're going. I don't much care where it is, as long as I'm with you, but I do want to know where I stand."

Galen smiled. "Maggie, there's never been anyone else for me but you. There never has been and there never will be. I'm pretty sure I know where we're going, but I want to give you a little more time to be perfectly sure. Does that answer your question?"

Maggie nodded, a surge of happiness flying through her. She flung her arms around Galen's neck and clung to him. It wasn't quite the answer she wanted, but it was close. She was sure, but considering the way she'd acted only yesterday, she couldn't blame him for being a little cautious.

"Maggie?" Galen whispered in her ear.

"What?"

"You're choking me." Galen laughed as Maggie quickly released him and pulled back. "Want to take off your clothes and get under the covers?" he asked.

"Yes," Maggie answered, smiling shyly.

"I'll help you, then," Galen said.

Moments later he sighed deeply in satisfaction as his eyes drank in the vision he had uncovered. "Lovely," he said. Then, with one hand he pulled the blanket down beneath her and flung it across her. He settled against his pillow, leaning on his elbow and watching her as she lay back and turned her head to look at him. "You're either going to have to lie still as a mouse over there, or you know what will happen," he said.

"I don't think my lying still will help much," Maggie said. She could feel the warmth of Galen's body across the short distance between them, and it called to her with an urgency that already had her trembling with desire. She turned on her side and moved closer, so entranced with Galen's eyes that she could not stop looking at them. Again, she touched his face, the lines that crinkled from the corners of his eyes, the strong angle of his cheekbone beneath, the tiny dark spot near one corner of his mouth.

She gasped as his arms moved to pull her close against him and she discovered that he had nothing on and his state of arousal was as great as her own. A torrent of joy and longing rushed through her. Soon she was to know the joy of belonging to him completely. But he slowed his quest, his eyes bright with happiness and laughter as he tickled her softly and she giggled in response. "Don't," she said and he clutched her to him, laughing. Together they rolled around on the bed like puppies at play, first one on top, then the other. Finally Galen stopped, with Maggie pinned beneath him.

"Oh, Maggie, darling, how I want you," he said hoarsely, darting little kisses around her face again.

"I want you, too," she replied, catching his head in both hands and cradling his face between them. "I'm yours, Galen," she whispered.

"I know," he said. Very slowly he rolled to one side, still holding her in his arms. "I think we'd better stop for now," he said, caressing her hair from her flushed face and smiling as she gave him a stricken look.

"Why?" she demanded, aching with need. "Why? Are you some kind of sadist? Are you trying to get even with me for yesterday?"

"No. I apologize for yesterday. I wasn't thinking clearly, I wanted you so badly. I had a long sleepless night to think it over and realize that I treated you like a brute. I want everything to be perfect between us, Maggie. Once we become lovers there'll be no turning back ever." He looked at Maggie seriously. "No turning back. Do you understand?"

"Of course I do!" she said impatiently. "But what's wrong with now? What makes you think I'd want to turn back?"

"Answer me this," he said, still teasing her face with tiny kisses. "If I'd come to you, say, a year ago and begged you to give it all up and come with me, would you have?"

"Stop it, Galen!" Maggie said, pushing him away. "This is no time for stupid questions. How do I know what I'd have done? You wouldn't have done that. It wouldn't have been you."

"But I thought about doing it," Galen said. "Many times. So answer me. Would you have?"

Maggie stared at him. Lord, if only she'd known. But if he *had* come to her a year ago, what would she have said? She had felt quite differently then, not so much about Galen, but about her life in general. She had learned a lot since then. "I don't really know, Galen," she said at last. "I might still have been very stupid. I don't know."

"Not stupid, Maggie," Galen said, taking her in his arms again. "Never you. But let's wait just a little longer, all right? It's not as if we're going to be separated ever again, unless you want it.''

"All right," Maggie said tightly, "but there's no chance that I will. We're going through all of this frustration for nothing."

Galen grinned. "Let's do something constructive about that. How about some bacon and eggs? I'm starving."

"In the middle of the night?" Maggie said, amazed at Galen's ability to recover and think about food so quickly.

"Why not? I'm a big boy and I need lots of feeding. That one little steak tonight wasn't nearly enough. I didn't have any lunch." With that he rolled out of bed and got to his feet.

Maggie sat and stared at him, the comforter clutched around her, while he began to get dressed. *What a magnificent body,* she thought, her fingers tingling with the desire to touch him again. Those broad shoulders, that flat stomach and narrow hips. There was little external evidence of the damage that caused his dependence on a cane, unless one looked and saw that he compensated by standing on the ball of one foot when the other was flat on the floor. He had obviously exercised hard to keep the muscles in the damaged leg from becoming withered.

Galen started to pull up his jeans, then looked over at her and cocked his head. "Is that lust I see in those gorgeous blue eyes?" he asked.

"You'd better believe it," she answered, smiling as Galen grinned at her and went back to dressing. "I think you're the sexiest man in the whole world," she added.

"And I think," Galen said, fastening his belt and putting his hands on his hips and grinning at her again, "that you not only know how to massage my shoulders, but my ego, as well." He bent and picked up Maggie's clothes from the floor. "Here," he said, tossing them to her. "Get dressed. I'm going to go and start cooking."

"What a man," Maggie murmured to his departing back. She dressed quickly, but by the time she reached the kitchen, Galen had already started the coffee and had a panful of bacon frying.

"Only coffee for me," Maggie said, moving close to him. "I'm still stuffed from dinner."

Galen put his arm around her and hugged her to him. "All right, but I intend to fatten you up just a little," he said, smiling at her. "I don't think a few more pounds would hurt you."

"You sound like my mother," Maggie said, making a face at him. Nevertheless, once they sat down at the table, she began to nibble on some toast and jam and ate two pieces of Galen's bacon. They talked endlessly, of everything that came into their minds, Galen finally telling Maggie about the case he had lost. It involved a bitter custody suit, Galen working on behalf of the father, who he felt was a much better-qualified parent.

"Unfortunately the judge didn't see it that way," he said grimly. "I feel sorry for those poor kids."

"They'll probably survive," Maggie said comfortingly. "Kids are amazingly tough. Look at little Carrie."

"I hope you're right," Galen said with a sigh.

The sun was coming up when Maggie finally began to yawn.

"You'd better take a nap before you drive home," Galen said. "I have to go into my office for a while, then

I'll be back around noon. I have to drive over to Spring Mountain later myself. We could go at the same time."

"You can come for dinner," Maggie said. "I'll call Mom and warn her."

"That sounds good," Galen said.

Maggie went to the telephone and dialed home. When she hung up a few minutes later, she was frowning and feeling decidedly anxious. "That's odd," she said, looking at Galen. "My mother was just going to call me. She said Bruce called and he wants me to come to Balfour Chemicals to see him at one o'clock. I wonder what he wants?"

Galen shrugged. "Probably just eager to try and counteract my influence," he said. "Why don't you go and curl up on my bed for a while? I'll wake you in time to go."

"I think I'll do that," Maggie agreed. "Wake me about noon."

Later, she thought that if she'd known what was going to happen, nothing in the world could have persuaded her to go.

CHAPTER NINE

IT WAS A FEW MINUTES before one when Maggie drove up to the gate in the high, barbed-wire-topped fence that surrounded Balfour Chemicals. She gave her name to the security guard. He directed her to the main administration building.

"I wouldn't come near this place if Bruce wasn't my brother," she muttered after she had parked and gotten out of her car. The very air smelled evil and filthy. Thank heaven she wouldn't be here long. Then she could drive home to Spring Mountain, where the air was clear, and Galen, who had gone on ahead, would be waiting for her. She took the elevator to the second floor as Bruce had directed, then walked halfway down a long carpeted corridor until she came to a reception area. A trim secretary, sitting at a sleek computer desk, looked up and smiled immediately.

"You're Ms. Preston, aren't you?" she said. When Maggie said yes, she flipped on an intercom. "Mr. Preston, your sister is here. Go right on in," she said, gesturing toward the door behind her.

Bruce opened the door before Maggie could reach it. "Hi, sis," he said, giving her a fleeting smile. "Come on in." He put his arm around Maggie's shoulders and led her to a chair close to his own, behind a massive teak desk. He sat down, picked up a pencil and began to tap it absently while he stared into space.

"Is something wrong?" Maggie asked. Bruce did not look frightened, but he did look tense.

Her brother's eyes met hers. "We've got a problem," he said.

"We?"

"Yes. Roger flew in this morning. He's still about ready to blow in six different directions because you told him you won't marry him. I still need more time, and I'm getting some pretty nasty threats about what Roger will do if I don't get you to see the light, so I had to promise I'd talk to you and get you to at least say you'd reconsider." Bruce raised his eyebrows and one corner of his mouth quirked nervously upward in an attempt at a smile. "So I'm asking you to tell Roger you'll do that, or—" he took a deep breath "—you may not have a brother."

"Oh, come on, Bruce," Maggie said, frowning. "Roger's not a murderer."

Bruce shook his head. "Maggie, you don't realize the state he's in. I doubt he'd do it himself, but he might well hire someone to do it."

Maggie stared at Bruce. The look Roger had given her when he'd left her apartment flashed into her memory. At that moment, he'd looked capable of killing, not in a moment of reckless passion, but coolly and deliberately. A shiver went through her, and she massaged her suddenly clammy fingertips. She still didn't understand where Bruce fit into all this. What did he need time for? No matter how terrible it was, she needed to know before she could even begin to think of doing what he asked. She chewed her lip pensively and leaned toward him.

"I'm sorry, Bruce, but I won't even consider it unless you tell me what's going on and why more time is going to solve your problem. I'm going to marry Galen, and that's final. I don't like the idea of that kind of deception. I'd rather hire bodyguards for you or send you someplace where you'd be safe.''

Bruce stared at her. Then he got up, walked quietly to his door and locked it. When he turned around, he was grinning from ear to ear and holding his arms out to Maggie.

Stunned, Maggie got up and went into his engulfing hug. ''I still don't understand!'' she said.

''Shh,'' Bruce whispered in her ear. ''Keep your voice down. God, that's great news. Did Galen propose to you last night?''

''Yes. Well, almost,'' Maggie said, baffled anew. ''How did you know?''

''Spies,'' Bruce said with a broad wink. He led her to her chair. ''Sit down and I'll tell you as much as I can in a few minutes.'' He leaned over and spoke on his intercom to his secretary. ''No calls, no nothing, from nobody,'' he said.

He turned to Maggie and bent forward, taking her hands in his. ''Okay, here's the story in a nutshell. It's still top secret, so keep that in the forefront of your mind. About a year ago, I discovered some tax fraud in the books that appeared to involve both the corporation and Roger personally. I took it to Galen. He told me the documentation we'd need to make both cases. We agreed to work together, and since some people knew we were old friends, take every opportunity to make it appear we were enemies. Before anyone could get suspicious about my snooping, I took the bull by the horns and told Roger I had the goods on him, but I'd cover it up and forget it since he was going to marry you. I thought at the time you were, and I didn't feel it was my place to interfere with your choice of a husband, even though Galen kept saying we ought to see if we could make you come to your senses. I asked for a few other goodies, like this job, so Roger would think I was really enough of a sleaze to do something that crooked. I called Galen some nasty names and told Roger that I thought he was basically a great guy and the perfect husband for you. It worked. Anyway, I really had him where it hurt, so he didn't have much choice.

"Meanwhile, Galen and I and . . . some other people kept at it, and when a lot more turned up, Galen and I agreed that we had to keep you from making the terrible mistake of marrying Roger." Bruce paused and grinned. "It was about then that I realized that Galen's concern for you wasn't just because you were my sister . . . anyway, somehow we had to keep you from deserting Roger completely until the investigation was completed and the grand jury had indicted him. If he thought I might spill what I knew, and he no longer had you to hold him here, he might skip the country. He's got millions stashed in the Caribbean. So Galen pulled one way and I pushed the other. Unfortunately Galen did a lot better job, and you made your decision a little too soon.

"Right now, a special grand jury is evaluating the evidence, and all our work will be for nothing if Roger doesn't hang around until it's finished. I don't think he has any idea yet, but he's worried. Especially since you're cozy with Galen. Apparently someone saw you at Galen's last night, playing with the puppies, and they said you were still there at midnight . . ."

"That telephone call!" Maggie exclaimed. At Bruce's questioning look, she told him about what she'd assumed was a wrong number. "Is Roger having me watched?" That idea sent cold chills racing through her already tense body.

"I wouldn't be surprised," Bruce replied. "Roger's so jealous he's fit to be tied. He made some pretty graphic statements about what he'd like to do to Galen. I can't convince him I'll stay in his corner even if you don't marry him, and I'm not sure he cares. Losing you was a terrible blow to his ego, and I think in his own strange way he really does love you. I don't think you'll be in any danger, or I'd never ask you to do this. If you'll give him a little encouragement, I don't think he'll leave, even though I think he's beginning to suspect that his days on top of the heap are numbered. So, will you help us?"

"Good Lord," Maggie said, her mind in a turmoil at what she had heard. It was like being caught in the middle of a spy thriller, without having read the first part. Not only had Bruce deceived Roger, but she had been completely fooled by both him and Galen. "You're some actor," she murmured.

Bruce grinned and shook his head. "Not quite good enough," he said. "My begging you to stick with Roger couldn't counteract the real thing from Galen. I thought I did a real academy-award job at the Red Duck, but it didn't faze you. Now it's your turn to try. Can you do it?"

Maggie sighed heavily. "I guess I'll have to," she replied. "I'll let him think I'm reconsidering, but that's *all* I'll do." She lifted her eyebrows meaningfully. "Understand?"

"Of course," Bruce said quickly. "Galen's going to hate having you even speak to the guy, but he'll go along when you tell him about it, because there isn't any choice."

"You tell him," Maggie said firmly. "I'm not going to open that particular can of worms and let Galen think I have any enthusiasm for it. You make it clear that you practically had to beat me to get me to do it."

"All right," Bruce agreed. "I'll talk to him tonight. Are you ready to see Roger?"

"Not really," Maggie replied. "I still don't like it. Just how serious is the indictment liable to be?"

"Maggie," Bruce said, looking into her eyes with intense seriousness, "Roger Balfour's whole empire is going to come crashing down. It's not a pretty story, and even I feel sorry for the guy." He squeezed her hands. "I'm just damned glad that you saw the light in time."

"So am I," Maggie said, shuddering. "Still, I'm sorry for Roger, too, in a way. He's such a pitiful, hollow person compared to Galen. I guess that will make it a little easier to pretend. Where is Roger?"

"He's waiting in the conference room down the hall for me to, quote, talk some sense into you, unquote. Are you ready? Shall we go?"

"I guess so," Maggie said slowly, "Though I don't think I'll ever be really ready for this."

"I understand," Bruce said. "Thanks, sis. You're the greatest."

Bruce took Maggie down the hall and opened the door to a luxurious conference room. Roger was sitting at the head of the table staring out the window. When Maggie entered, he turned quickly toward her and got up, trying to give her a welcoming smile. His lips curved, but his eyes remained wary. "Hello, Maggie," he said softly.

"Hello, Roger," she said, making an effort to smile at him. "I... I'm sorry to hear you've been so upset." She glanced at Bruce, who gave her an encouraging smile. "Bruce has convinced me that I ought to... give you another chance. I'm not ready to reverse my decision, but I'll reconsider."

Roger's face broke into a genuine smile. "That's wonderful. That's more than I'd hoped for. Bruce, you're a marvel." He came toward Maggie, his arms outstretched, and she let him take her into his arms and hold her close. Her arms closed around him, and she leaned her cheek against his, breathing the familiar scent of his after-shave and sighing. What a pitiful complicated story it had turned out to be. And the saddest part of all was that Roger, in his own subdued and selfish way, really thought he loved her.

"I'll leave you two alone," Bruce said, and Maggie heard him go out and close the door behind him.

"Shall we sit down and talk for a while?" she suggested to Roger. "I'm due at home a little later, but I'm not in a hurry."

While they talked, Maggie could see that Roger was making a real effort to respond to her complaints about their relationship, telling her in some detail of a business trip he'd just made to the Netherlands. What might have happened, she wondered sadly, if he had included her that way in the past? When she finally told him that she had to leave, he at first looked angry, then his face brightened.

"I'll come with you," he said. "I think I should try to make a better impression on your parents. I've got a car, and I can have my plane fly over to Beckley to pick me up later."

"I . . . don't think that would be a good idea," Maggie said. Good Lord, if he should go and find Galen there, the fireworks would really begin and her attempt to string him along would be for nothing. Not to mention what Galen would think if she showed up with Roger in tow before Bruce had a chance to talk to him! "My mother hates to have company when she hasn't had time to clean the house," she added lamely.

Roger's eyes narrowed. "You wouldn't be planning to get together with Kendrick again tonight, would you?" he asked, his voice icy.

"Oh, no!" Maggie said quickly.

"Good. Because I'd hate to think that you were only stringing me along to please your brother, while you and Kendrick were having a fine old fling on the side. So why don't you call your mother and warn her I'm coming? She'll have plenty of time to dust before we get there."

"All right," Maggie agreed. She could stop in Bruce's office and have him call right away, to warn Galen about what had happened and tell him not to be there.

Roger followed her into Bruce's office. "Roger, I need to talk to Bruce alone," Maggie said, frowning at him.

"And I need to hear you make that phone call," Roger said, eyeing her skeptically.

"No, you don't!" Maggie was suddenly so angry and frustrated at being put in this situation that she could barely contain herself. She took Roger by the shoulders and pushed him toward the door. "If you don't trust me any more than that, forget everything I said! It will never work!" She put her hands on his face and gave him a quick kiss on the lips. "Get out!"

"Yes, Maggie," Roger said, smiling. "I always did love your hot Irish temper."

As soon as the door closed, Maggie bent and whispered her problem into Bruce's ear. He nodded.

"Don't worry, I'll take care of it," he replied softly. "It's best to keep Galen away from him completely and not let Roger think you're too interested in him. God knows what Roger might do if he knew the truth about you two."

"Thanks," Maggie said, grimacing. "Here goes nothing."

She rejoined Roger, who was standing close to the door.

"I didn't hear you talking on the phone," he said, his expression cold and suspicious again.

"The line was busy, and I didn't feel like waiting," Maggie replied without flinching. "Mother sometimes talks for hours. She'll just have to put up with the consequences." How easy it was, she thought bitterly, to become a glib liar. Oh, well, it was for a good reason.

Maggie led the way to Spring Mountain, driving as slowly as she could to give Galen plenty of time to get to her parents' house and receive Bruce's message. All the while, she kept trying to digest the fact that Bruce and Galen had been working together and she had never had a clue. Or had she? Shouldn't she have been suspicious when they both began casting aspersions on Roger's character? At the overdone ferocity of their conflict? No, she decided with a sigh, they had both been so clever that she really believed they were at each other's throats. Bruce had done an especially good job, since he'd had to pretend to be on exactly the opposite side from where his sentiments lay. She only hoped that she could do as well, and that she wouldn't have to do it for very long.

When she reached Spring Mountain, Maggie glanced at her watch. The trip had taken a good two hours. Plenty of time for Bruce to talk to Galen. Nevertheless, when she turned the corner into the cul-de-sac, her heart was pounding. When she saw that Galen's car was in her parents' driveway, sheer fear took over and her teeth began to chatter. Had Bruce failed to reach him, or had Galen stayed, from some perverse desire to confront Roger Balfour? That didn't make sense. Not with so much at stake. If he hadn't heard from Bruce, how could she get him aside and tell him why she had Roger with her? And what, in God's name, could she do to prevent some kind of terrible scene when Roger discovered that Galen was here?

Very slowly, Maggie got out of her car, her mind clicking along in a dream world where everything was crystal clear, but her body felt as if it didn't belong to her. She moved rapidly to Roger's side as he got out of his rented Mercedes.

"Roger," she said, taking a firm grip on his arm and fixing him with an intense look, "I have to make something very clear to you." She gestured toward Galen's car. "That is Galen Kendrick's car. I know you hate him, but he is a dear friend of my parents. He visits them often. They think of him as a second son. So you better be nice to him if you want to score any points with Mom and Dad. Do you understand?" While she spoke, she saw Roger's expression go from one of violent anger to an almost blank stare. He had understood.

"Very well," he said tightly, "but I hope he doesn't plan to stay around. I don't know how long I can pretend to be pleasant to him."

"I doubt he will," Maggie said dryly. In fact, if he thought she had really had second thoughts, he might well leave in moments. If so, she could only hope that Bruce would finally reach him and explain what had happened.

Clinging to Roger's arm for support more than anything, Maggie accompanied him to the front door and knocked. "Smile," she ordered Roger, who was looking increasingly grim.

The moment the door opened, he looked at her and actually laughed.

"Well...hello," said Mrs. Preston, her eyebrows leaping in surprise. "I, uh, that is, we—"

"I know, Mom," Maggie said, kissing her cheek swiftly. "Roger happened to be at Balfour Chemicals today when I stopped by to see Bruce, and he wanted to come and say hello before he went back to New York."

"It was a beautiful day for a drive through the mountains," Roger said affably, following Maggie into the living room.

The scene that greeted Maggie's eyes was a familiar one. Her father was seated in his favorite lounge chair, Galen sprawled comfortably in a chair beside him. The moment he saw Roger, Maggie knew that Bruce had not talked to him. His expression went from warm to frigid in an instant, the look he gave her a combination of white-hot anger and heartbreaking betrayal.

"What in hell is he doing here?" he demanded, getting quickly to his feet while he kept his eyes fixed intently on Maggie's.

"Well, when I w-went to see Bruce..." Maggie stammered. She stopped, a wave of dizziness sweeping over her at the stark anguish she saw in Galen's eyes. She clutched at Roger's arm, trying desperately to breathe and keep her body functioning.

"Maggie and I had a little talk," Roger put in smoothly. "She's decided that maybe I'm not such a bad sort, after all. It might be better for you to take a different tone with her. I think you're upsetting her." He slipped a protective arm around Maggie's shoulders and hugged her.

"*I* am upsetting *her?*" Galen said scathingly. His narrowed eyes swept from Maggie's frightened face to Roger's deliberately placid expression, then he gave a short, dry laugh. "You two make a charming couple." His eyes raked them again, then rested on Maggie, now two cold, impenetrable spots of gray beneath his heavy black brows. "Both masters of deception."

He turned and picked up his cane. "I think I'd better leave. I'm sure my company isn't welcome." He gave a curt nod to Maggie and Roger. "Have a nice evening," he said, his voice dripping with sarcasm. He said a courteous goodbye to Maggie's parents, then went out the door without a backward glance.

Locked onto Roger's arm, Maggie stood still as a rock, trying desperately not to burst into tears and give away the terrible anguish she felt. It was obvious that Galen believed the worst of her, but for his sake she had to try to act as normal as possible. She felt Roger's eyes on her and turned slowly to look at him.

"I apologize for Galen's temper," she said tightly. "He's so involved in his causes that he's not very tolerant."

Roger looked at her thoughtfully. "I understand," he said. "It puts you in a very difficult position. I'm sorry."

Tears sprang to Maggie's eyes. In that moment, she felt a stronger affection for Roger than she ever had before, and a deeper sorrow at the knowledge of the fate that awaited him. If he only knew how difficult her position was! She leaned over and kissed his cheek. "That's sweet of you, Roger," she said huskily. "I'll go and help Mom with dinner. Why don't you and Dad have a nice talk?"

Maggie fled to the kitchen, where her mother immediately accosted her with a hissed, "Margaret, what ever possessed you to bring that man here today?"

"Sh!" Maggie warned her. "I will not have you insulting Roger. He's still my friend." She put her mouth next to her mother's ear and whispered. "Were you on the phone all afternoon?"

Mrs. Preston frowned. "No, the telephone is out of order. Some fool with a backhoe cut the main line into Spring Mountain. They won't have it repaired until tomorrow morning. Why?"

"Never mind," Maggie replied, her heart sinking. Not only had Galen not gotten Bruce's message, but she would be unable to reach him and tell him the truth once Roger had gone. Of course, she could drive to a neighboring town and try to call, or go to Charleston to see him. That would be better than waiting and hoping that Bruce finally succeeded in reaching him.

Those plans were demolished before dinner was over. Roger, as warm and charming as Maggie had ever seen him, was making real headway with her father, and even her mother gave him a grudging smile or two when he complimented her cooking. When he suddenly realized that he had forgotten to call the Charleston airport and tell his pilot to fly to Beckley to meet him and then learned the telephone was out of order, Mr. Preston invited him to spend the night.

Roger fairly glowed. "Why, thank you," he said. "I'd like that very much." He beamed at Maggie. "Fate is sometimes very kind, isn't it?" he said.

"Yes, I guess it is," Maggie said. Inside, she felt a sense of guilt that almost tore her apart. Her heart ached for Roger, for Galen and for herself. A master of deception, Galen had called her. She was doing it well, but how she hated it. The only shred of comfort she could grasp at was the fact that Roger had been practicing the art for much longer than she, and it had not bothered his conscience at all.

In the morning, Roger seemed so distraught at leaving her that Maggie redoubled her efforts to convince him she was not planning an illicit affair with Galen in his absence.

"I am not available for that kind of thing, and you know it!" she told him severely. "I'll see you in New York next week. I'm going to stop in Philadelphia on the way to see a dear little girl, the daughter of some old friends of mine, who is undergoing a last-resort treatment for leukemia. If you want to worry about something, worry about her. The doctor told me she needs a miracle."

Roger sighed. "I guess I should count my blessings, shouldn't I? I've had more luck than I deserved." He held Maggie close and looked into her eyes. "Whatever happens, Maggie," he said softly, "remember that I love you."

Maggie put her arms around him and pressed her cheek briefly to his. He knew something terrible was about to happen, or sensed it somehow, she thought. Perhaps, deep inside, he knew that she would never really change her mind and marry him. "Have a safe trip, Roger," she said quietly. "I'll see you soon."

As soon as Roger had gone, Maggie hurried into the kitchen to call Galen. Her mother was hovering by the sink, pretending to busy herself rearranging some glassware in the dish drainer.

"Mother, please, would you mind leaving me alone while I make a couple of phone calls?" Maggie asked plaintively. "The next thing this house is going to get is a telephone in every room so people can have some privacy." As soon as her mother had left, grumbling about some people who had the kind of business they didn't want other people to know about, Maggie dialed Galen's office.

"Mr. Kendrick is out of town for the rest of this week," his secretary told Maggie in clipped tones. "He left word that you were to see another attorney, Walter Pratt, about your foundation. He sent some papers over to him."

"Where did Mr. Kendrick go?" Maggie asked.

"I don't know exactly," the secretary replied. "He said he'd be deep-sea fishing on a friend's boat in the Florida Keys. Is there anything else?"

"No. I guess not," Maggie said. Damn! It sounded very much as if Bruce had not contacted Galen. Was he really out of town, or did he just not want to speak to her? She had better find out from Bruce before she let herself get too agitated.

When Bruce's secretary answered, Maggie suddenly realized that it might not be a good idea for her to mention Galen's name in her conversation, in case someone overheard what she said. As soon as Bruce came on the line, Maggie said, "Hi, Bruce. Were you ever able to contact the party we talked about yesterday?"

"I'm afraid not, Maggie," he replied. "I tried several times last night, but he wasn't in. I wouldn't worry about it, though. He's smart enough to figure out what's going on."

"I didn't see any sign that he was," Maggie said bitterly.

There was a short pause, then Bruce sighed. "All I can say is, don't worry about it."

"Don't worry about it! If you'd been there..." Maggie choked to a stop, a sob clogging her throat.

"Stop it, Maggie," Bruce said gruffly. "When are you going back to New York?"

"A...a week from tomorrow. Why?" Maggie replied, frowning at the telephone. Bruce certainly wasn't very sympathetic.

"I think you should go back by this Friday at the latest. It would make Roger feel a lot better. Why don't you call him later and tell him that you'd like him to send a plane for you?"

Maggie dashed the tears from her cheeks impatiently. That was all she needed! An invitation to spend more time deceiving Roger. She was about to say she was darned if she would when it occurred to her that Bruce might have a special reason for his request. He had sounded very serious.

"Why Friday?" she demanded.

"I could come with you," Bruce replied. "I'm about due for a break, and a few days in the big city sounds good right now."

"All right," Maggie said with a sigh. "I'll see if I can arrange it and call you back."

"Gee, sis, don't sound so excited about having my company," Bruce teased. "The other girls tell me I'm lots of fun."

"Ha, ha," Maggie replied. She was supposed to sound excited while poor Galen was off somewhere on a fishing boat, probably dragging in fish after fish and pretending each one was her as he beheaded it? Men and their games. Sometimes she hated them. All she wanted was for this whole disastrous deception to be over so she could curl up in the comfort of Galen's arms and tell him she loved him and never, ever, see that look of pain in his beautiful eyes again.

CHAPTER TEN

IT WAS NOT UNTIL the next day, after Maggie had seen the attorney, Walter Pratt, and made some temporary arrangements to get funds to the Bryants, that she began to wonder if there wasn't something very fishy about Galen's fishing trip. As she made plans for funding the foundation, she realized she would not be able to put her brownstone on the market until the grand jury had finished its work and she no longer needed to keep up her painful pretense. Galen was doubtless involved in presenting the material implicating Roger and his cohorts to the grand jury. That could well be where he was; also the reason for his sudden absence. She had no idea where the grand jury might be meeting, but she was at least a little relieved to think that he had not gone off to brood about her duplicity. She thought Bruce would be needed at the hearings, too. Of course it was possible that he was, but at a different time. Those two were smart enough to arrange things so that they wouldn't both be making suspicious trips out of town at the same time.

When she and Bruce were on their way to the airport on Friday morning, she asked him point blank if the Keys were where Galen really was.

"You're getting smarter all the time," Bruce replied with a grin.

"Aren't you going to have to appear before the grand jury, too?" Maggie asked next.

"I already did," Bruce said.

"Already? When? Where?"

Bruce shook his head. "Can't say. All I can say is that when the federal government wants something to be secret, they really know how to do it. You won't see Galen again until it's over, but if anyone were to investigate, they'd find he's gone fishing in the Keys."

Maggie groaned. "I've heard of those grand-jury investigations going on for months. I don't think I can stand it."

"This isn't that kind," Bruce said quickly. "All the materials and witnesses are already rounded up. The counts for indictment are specified. All the grand jury has to do is evaluate each one, and it shouldn't take long. The federal prosecutor that Galen's been working with says he can't find any loose ends, and I doubt the jury will, either. Galen's brilliant." Bruce reached over and squeezed Maggie's hand. "That's quite a guy you've got."

"I hope I've still got him," Maggie said sadly. "I'm afraid that even if he did figure out what happened, he might think I was a little too eager to be nice to Roger again."

"No, he won't," Bruce said. "He knows you. He'll understand."

Tears came to Maggie's eyes. "I guess maybe you're right. But it doesn't make me like what I have to do any better."

"You're not supposed to like it," Bruce said. "You have a conscience that watches every move you make. Roger's only covers what he wants it to cover." He squeezed Maggie's hand again. "Come on, perk up. By the time we get to Philadelphia, you've got to look happy for Carrie, remember?"

"Don't worry, I'll manage," Maggie promised. "I can't let her down."

But when Maggie and Bruce entered the forbiddingly complex world of the intensive care unit where Carrie lay, Maggie had difficulty following through on her promise to be cheerful. It looked like a place where people went in, but seldom went out.

"How is she today?" she asked the special nurse who met them at the entrance to Carrie's cubicle. Her heart sank as the nurse pursed her thin lips and looked down at the chart she held in her hand.

"I think," the nurse said cautiously, "that I have just recorded some positive signs. I am about to call Dr. Grant."

"Wonderful!" Maggie said. Now she did feel like smiling. She went into the room where the Bryants were watching over their little girl and gave them both a hug before she turned to Carrie. Seeing her lying there, so pale and small in her maze of tubes and monitors, Maggie's smile almost faded, but the dazzling brightness of Carrie's smile gave her the heart to be strong.

"You're doing just great, love," she told her, holding the tiny cold hand in hers.

"I'm feeling better today," Carrie said. "I know I look awful, but I really do feel better."

"That's the best news I ever heard," Maggie said. "I know Galen will be very happy, too. I couldn't bring him with me today, but I brought my brother, Bruce." She beckoned to Bruce, who was standing in the doorway. "Come and meet Carrie."

Maggie and Bruce were allowed to stay for only a few minutes. Afterward, the young Dr. Grant told them that, indeed, Carrie did show signs of responding, but it was still too early to tell anything about the eventual out-come.

"I'll call every day, if you don't mind," Maggie said.

"Call as often as you like," Dr. Grant replied. "It means a lot to Carrie, and to all of us."

During the short flight to New York, Maggie was silent, meditating about the strange series of events that had led her to this point in her life, when only a few months ago she had been on an entirely different track. It seemed almost unreal, a play within a play that would end and then her other life would resume. Roger met them at the airport, greeted Maggie with a tender kiss and immediately inquired about the little girl she had stopped to see.

"I'm so glad," he said, when Maggie told him there was now a glimmer of hope. She wondered what he would have thought if he knew the whole story.

To Maggie's surprise, Silverton was at his usual post. The threat of a lawsuit must have given Roger second thoughts, she mused, wondering again what he would think of her involvement in that crisis. No wonder she felt as if she was living in a dream world! She was trying to lead two different lives. If only it would end and she could see Galen again. One life with him was all she wanted.

The trancelike feeling persisted. On one level she was having a quietly pleasant time with Roger, dining and dancing at familiar haunts where the tasteful elegance was never intruded upon by the more sordid events outside. On another, she could almost envision a spring inside her winding tighter and tighter as each day passed. When Bruce left on Tuesday, still assuring her she had nothing to worry about as far as Galen was concerned, she felt like bursting into tears of frustration. How did he know? He hadn't seen Galen's face when she appeared on Roger's arm.

Wednesday passed, then Thursday. On Friday, Roger was to pick Maggie up at four o'clock to drive to Connecticut to visit some old friends for a couple of days at their country home. Maggie dreaded the weekend, but packed a small suitcase and, when the time came, was waiting in a new ivory-colored pantsuit with a jade-green silk camisole blouse. When Roger had not arrived by four-thirty, she became annoyed. He usually called when he was going to be delayed. By five o'clock, she was fuming. She threw her suit jacket on a chair, turned on the television news channel and flopped down on her sofa to watch. As luck would have it, the same commercial with bouncing suntanned teenagers that Galen had hated was showing.

"I hate it, too," Maggie muttered. What right did those brats have to be so happy when she was so miserable?

The commercial ended and a female anchor appeared, smiling brightly. "Good evening," she said. "The top story this Friday night is stunning news from the world of corporate high rollers. This afternoon a special federal grand jury in New York handed down a twenty-two-count indictment against Roger Balfour of Balfour Chemicals, shown here being led away by federal marshalls. Other officials of the giant corporation were also indicted..."

Maggie's heart almost stopped beating. There, on the screen, she saw Roger, handcuffed, an officer on either side of him, being led away from the building where his offices were. He looked straight at the camera, his expression dazed, as if he, too, suddenly found himself in a world that was not real. Tears came to Maggie's eyes and rolled silently down her cheeks. It was over. With a great sigh of relief, she bowed her head and closed her eyes. Now if only she could find Galen, if only he had understood...

The doorbell rang and she looked up. Reporters already? she wondered grimly. "Anna," she called, "tell whoever it is that I'm not—"

She stopped, staring, her heart suddenly beating wildly. There, standing at the entrance to her living room, looking rumpled and tired, stood Galen.

"Galen!" Maggie got to her feet and went toward him, smiling through her tears. He looked gaunt and exhausted, and his expression was so tense and drawn that she could not tell if he was happy or sorry to see her. He took only a step or two in her direction, then came to a halt, watching her closely. Gradually his face broke into that wide beautiful smile she loved. He held out his arms and Maggie flew into them, clinging to him and laughing and crying at the same time.

"Maggie, baby, thank God," he said, showering her face with kisses. He took her face between his hands, shaking his head and blinking back the tears that brimmed in his eyes. "Is it really all right? Are you still mine?"

"Of course!" Maggie cried, pulling his head down and kissing his lips. "Mmm, you taste so good," she said, kissing him again and again. "Is it really over? Is it really all over?"

"It really is," Galen said softly.

Maggie took hold of his arm. "Come and sit down and tell me about it," she said. "You look exhausted." She led him to the sofa and curled up beside him, nestled in his arms. "I feel as if a huge heavy weight that

I've been carrying around for weeks has just been taken away," she said, smiling into the warmth of his eyes.

"So do I," Galen said. He took a deep breath and sighed heavily. "I expected to feel a lot more elated when it happened than I do."

"I understand," Maggie said, caressing the line of his jaw with her forefinger. "I feel the same way. I've been expecting it, but it was still a terrible shock, seeing him taken away in handcuffs."

"I know." Galen's voice was deep and tender against Maggie's ear as he bent his head to nuzzle it with his lips, his arms warm and comforting around her. "I tried to get here before you found out that way. However you felt about me, I didn't want you to face it alone."

Maggie raised her face to his and smiled wistfully. "It doesn't make sense, does it? There were times I would have thought seeing Roger sent to prison would make me jump for joy, but when Bruce told me that he really would be, I felt sorry for him."

Galen nodded. "So did I, in a way. It's not pleasant to destroy a man, any man. Even worse, I knew what you'd been asked to do, and I was afraid that with that big soft heart of yours you'd begin to feel more and more sorry for him. I even imagined you'd start to think that he needed you more than I did, after the way I left you that day at your parents'."

He laid his hand along Maggie's cheek, then brushed her hair back gently. "I've cursed myself over and over for that," he said. "It took me a few minutes after you came in with Roger to realize what must have happened, but I couldn't find any way to let you know. I tried to tell you that I knew you were deceiving everyone, but I could tell you didn't understand. Then I got the call that same night that I had to leave, and since then there's been no chance for me to tell you or have anyone else tell you for me. Bruce and I were forbidden to have any contact.''

"Bruce told me you'd understand," Maggie said, "but I was never sure. I've been worried all this time that you'd hate me because I'd let you down so terribly. I wouldn't do that, Galen, not ever.''

Galen smiled, the lines of tension suddenly leaving his face, replaced by pure sunshine sparkling from the depths of his eyes. "Do you mind if I give one more huge sigh of relief?" he asked, then proceeded to do so before he pulled Maggie onto his lap and held her even more tightly against him. "God, but it's good to hold you," he said, covering her face with kisses again. "I swear, sometimes this week my arms have ached from wanting so much to be able to hold you and know you were still mine."

"My whole body has ached from wanting to be in your arms," Maggie said, burrowing closer to him. "It's the only place where I ever feel perfectly happy."

"Oh, Maggie, my darling." Galen's voice was husky with emotion as he lifted her chin gently with his fingers, his eyes bright with happiness. "I love you so much," he said. "I should have told you before, but it's so hard to say it when you're afraid your dream may never come true."

"I love you, too," Maggie whispered. She clung to Galen as his mouth descended on hers, sweeping away all the unhappiness of the past with a passion that left her breathless and left no doubt in her mind that he was hers forever.

He raised his head and took a ragged breath. "Is there somewhere we could go to talk about my dream?" he asked. "Somewhere where I can hold you and love you the way I've wanted to since… Well, that story can wait, too."

He smiled as Maggie slid from his lap and took his hand and began leading him toward the stairs, her face radiant.

"I know just the place," she said. "That bedroom you asked about one night not long ago."

Galen paused at the bottom of the stairs. "Ah, yes," he said. He turned and looked at Maggie's luxurious living room. "This is really beautiful," he said. "I hadn't noticed. All I've seen is you since I came in the door. But this is the kind of place I'd imagined you lived in." He smiled at Maggie. "You see, I've had a dream for a long time. Do you mind if I carry you up the stairs? That's been part of the dream. These may not be the exact stairs I dreamed about, but they'll do."

"Of course I don't mind," Maggie said, holding fast to Galen's neck as he tucked her against him with one strong arm.

"There," he said, as he carefully started up the stairs. His eyes sparked mischief at her. "I even practiced carrying things up my stairs so I'd be sure not to drop you. Of course, until you came to my house that night, I didn't think I'd ever get to carry you, but it was good exercise."

Maggie laughed and kissed his cheek. "What's this all about? You sound as if you've been planning it for years."

"I have. I told you there's never been anyone else for me," Galen said. "Now hush and listen to my story."

"Yes, darling love," Maggie said meekly.

Galen laughed. "That's better. Once upon a time, long ago, when I was an ugly crippled boy, a beautiful princess came into my life. She made the sun shine again and the flowers bloom, and I loved her with all my heart. But, as princesses will, she went on to royal things, leaving the ugly crippled boy behind. Doctors worked their magic, and he wasn't so ugly or crippled anymore. By then, the princess was far away, living in a beautiful palace of her own where people bowed before her and worshiped her every day. She had taken the boy's heart with her. It was hers to keep forever, and even though the boy grew into a man and knew it was foolish, he still imagined that some day the princess would return. One look and she would fall in love with him. Then he would sweep her onto his magnificent steed, ride with her to his castle and carry her through the door to a bower filled with flowers. Soon, they would be married and live happily ever after.''

Galen stopped at the top of the stairs. ''I never really believed that dream would come true,'' he said, his eyes scanning Maggie's face adoringly.

''And now it has,'' Maggie whispered, blinking back the mist of love that filled her eyes. ''What a lovely dream, Galen. But I'm not a princess. I'm just the girl who's loved you all along but didn't know it because the princess thing got in the way.''

''You'll always be my princess,'' Galen said. He looked at Maggie, his eyes sparkling with mischief. ''And now, lovely one,'' he said, ''I think it's time we started making up for lost time. We have a lot to talk about, but I am going insane with wanting you, and it will take weeks for our families to put together the kind of royal wedding we deserve. I'll wait if you want to, but it will have to be in a padded cell.''

''Heaven forbid,'' Maggie said, laughing.

Galen smiled. ''In that case, which door is the bower?''

"The white double doors straight ahead," Maggie replied nestling contentedly against Galen's shoulder as he opened them and carried her through.

SOME TIME LATER, as Maggie lay in the warmth of Galen's arms, her months of longing at last assuaged, she sighed dreamily and said, "I think we should spend the rest of our lives right here. Anna can bring us some food now and then and the rest of the time we'll make love. What could be more perfect?"

Galen laughed and hugged her closer. "Wouldn't that be wonderful! Too bad the real world will catch up with us eventually, isn't it?"

Maggie sighed. "Yes. I've had enough reality lately. Although a lot of the time, I felt as if nothing was real at all. It wasn't much fun leading a double life, when the only one I wanted was here, with you."

"Poor baby," Galen said softly, kissing her forehead. "I know it wasn't easy, but without your help, we might not have succeeded. Roger might have left if you hadn't, because of what he knew Bruce knew, but our worst fear was that he'd do something rash. I think once you told him you wouldn't marry him, he suddenly faced the prospect of a life alone in another country, an exile who could never return, and hated it. Under those circumstances a man with the kind of power Roger had can be much more dangerous than someone as kind and loving as you are would suspect."

"That's what Bruce told me," Maggie said. She shook her head and smiled wryly. "I wonder if Roger would believe that I hated to deceive him. I'm almost sure he suspected all along. Would you mind if I wrote him a note and told him sometime soon?"

"Of course not," Galen said softly. "You wouldn't be you if you didn't feel that way." He shifted Maggie in his arms and began to stroke her back gently with his hand. "We're going to have a long happy life together, Maggie. We won't have a lot of things. There are always more places that money is needed than any amount I could possibly make. I used to worry that you'd find life with me rather drab after what you've had here, but as soon as you came up with your idea for a foundation, I knew you wouldn't mind."

"Life with you drab?" Maggie raised her head and kissed Galen's chin. "Never. There are so many things to do, things we both care about. I'll at least help run the foundation. And maybe, when the children are in school, I'll go back to school and get a law degree, too. Could you use a partner?"

Galen laughed. "Wait a minute there, back up. How many children are we going to have? My dream never got that far."

Maggie smiled. "Three or four?"

"Sounds reasonable," Galen agreed. "And if you can find time to get a law degree, I can't think of anything I'd like more than to have you as my partner there, too." He pulled Maggie closer again, molding her against his length. "Babies right away?" he whispered in her ear.

"Yes, definitely," she replied, caressing him so that he groaned in delight. "Let's make love again, and then call our families and tell them to start planning a wedding."

IT WAS A WARM AFTERNOON in early June when Maggie and Galen repeated their vows beneath a huge spreading maple tree on the wide green lawn at Haven Hill. Hundreds of folding chairs ringed the flower-bedecked altar. Almost everyone in the little town of Spring

Mountain was there. Friends had come from every part of West Virginia, from New York and a dozen other states. As Maggie, radiant in an old-fashioned bridal gown of the softest chiffon and lace, moved down the aisle between the rows of chairs, she thought her heart would burst with happiness. Everyone she loved was there. Her father was well enough to escort her to the altar, where Galen waited, more handsome in his formal attire than any prince she could have imagined. Bruce, grinning from ear to ear, was at his side as best man.

But waiting with them was someone almost more special. Wearing a pink gown and a bonnet of flowers was her little maid of honor. Carrie Bryant, still frail-looking but with a touch of color in her cheeks, filled Maggie with the strong hope she was on the way to recovery.

"This was a perfect day," Maggie said to Galen, when hours later they were at last alone at his home, curled up together on the sofa, surrounded by stacks of gifts and slowly opening the mountain of cards from well-wishers. "Look at this. Even a card from the federal prosecutor."

"He's a nice guy," Galen said. "You'd like him." He tossed the rest of the cards he was holding onto the table and stretched luxuriously. "Well, Mrs. Kendrick, what say we go to bed? It's getting late, and we want to get an early start for the Keys in the morning."

"I'm ready." Maggie stood up and put her arms around Galen's neck. "Are you going to carry me upstairs again before I get too heavy?" she asked, giving him a smug little smile.

"Too heavy?" Galen stared at her blankly, then burst into joyous laughter. "Already? Are you sure?"

Maggie nodded. "Positive."

Galen kissed her passionately. "I'll carry both of you up as long as I can," he said, and swept her into his arms.

HARLEQUIN PROUDLY PRESENTS A DAZZLING CONCEPT IN ROMANCE FICTION

One small town,
twelve terrific love stories

JOIN US FOR A YEAR IN THE FUTURE OF TYLER

Each book set in Tyler is a self-contained love story; together,
the twelve novels stitch the fabric of the community.

LOSE YOUR HEART TO TYLER!

Join us for the second TYLER book, BRIGHT HOPES, by
Pat Warren, available in April.

*Former Olympic track star Pam Casals arrives in Tyler to
coach the high school team. Phys ed instructor Patrick
Kelsey is first resentful, then delighted. And rumors fly about
the dead body discovered at the lodge.*

Following the success of **WITH THIS RING**, Harlequin cordially invites you to enjoy the romance of the wedding season with

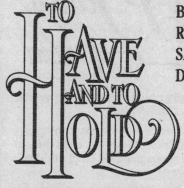

BARBARA BRETTON
RITA CLAY ESTRADA
SANDRA JAMES
DEBBIE MACOMBER

A collection of romantic stories that celebrate the joy, excitement, and mishaps of planning that special day by these four award-winning Harlequin authors.

Available in April at your favorite Harlequin retail outlets.

THTH

Janet Dailey
Americana

Janet Dailey's perennially popular Americana series continues with more exciting states!

Don't miss this romantic tour of America through fifty favorite Harlequin Presents novels, each one set in a different state, and researched by Janet and her husband, Bill.

A journey of a lifetime in one cherished collection.

April titles   **#29 NEW HAMPSHIRE**
Heart of Stone

#30 NEW JERSEY
One of the Boys
